A DEMON AND HIS WITCH

WELCOME TO HELL #1

EVE LANGLAIS

Copyright © June 2012, Eve Langlais

Cover Art Dreams2Media July 2017

Produced in Canada

Published by Eve Langlais

www.EveLanglais.com

E-ISBN: 978-1-927459-03-4

Print ISBN: 978-1-988328-71-3

KDP ISBN: 978-1499198805

PROLOGUE

A LONG, long time ago…

I'M GOING TO DIE. AND PAINFULLY, TOO, WHICH REALLY wasn't how she'd pictured spending her day. Gardening, yes. Maybe whipping up a few healing potions. Fooling around with her lover. Getting roasted to a crisp while the townsfolk looked on cheering? Not something she would have fit in to her schedule.

Ysabel pulled at the rope binding her to the stake, her mind still cloudy with disbelief. When she woke this morning and went about her chores, feeding the hens and collecting their eggs, tending her herb garden and other mundane tasks, she never expected a mob to descend upon her screaming, "Brujería! Witch!"

The fact they were correct didn't surprise her. She'd never tried too hard to hide her healing powers. Besides, the whole village benefitted from her concoctions which she used in exchange for items she needed. Smoked ham for a gout cure. A wheel of cheese for a tincture to soften chapped skin. Love potions by the handful for hopeful maidens and their mamas – a lucrative trade for a woman like herself without a husband or father to care for her. As for her title of witch, while she heard it bandied about, she didn't take offense. She was proud of her heritage handed down, generation after generation, by the women of her family. What shocked her when the screams to string her up and roast her came to her ears, was who headed the mob – her lover's mother, Luysa.

Dressed in a heavy black gown, her mantilla of black lace pulled back to show eyes burning with hatred and lips curled in a vicious snarl, she screamed "Burn the witch!" loudest.

Shriveled old hag. It seemed someone didn't want to cut the apron strings to her only son. Yet, Francisco, at twenty and five, was well past the age to settle down and begin his own line. A family he'd promised to build with her. While they met in secret due to his strict mother, and the village gossips, he'd promised to soon publicly announce his intent to wed her. She couldn't wait, although, now confronted with his angry mother, she wondered if they should have spoken sooner.

Ysabel didn't put up much of a fight. Why bother when she couldn't win against the number of folk sent to fetch her? Limp in their grasp, she closed her eyes and mind to their vicious taunts as they dragged her off to the edge of town where the narrow minded village people showed themselves busy, erecting a wooden stake and piling bramble and branches around it. Even as they lashed her to the pole, she didn't panic. Francisco, her lover with his dark eyes and thick lashes, would save her. Evidently, he'd told his mother of their love, and she'd temporarily lost her temper – and mind. Yet, Ysabel knew the man she loved would come to her rescue. Their commitment to each other would prevail over the mob's need to execute a witch as the church and religious heads in Rome instructed them.

As the villagers continued to pile flammable items about her and the sun began its descent, signaling the arrival of nightfall, she held on to that belief, clung firmly to her love as the first torch approached, its flickering flame dancing in the light breeze. Despite the situation, the scene was almost picturesque, reminding her of the many bonfires she'd participated in, with these same folk, as they celebrated the harvest and the solstices. Of course, nobody was lashed to the stake on those occasions. *Lucky me.*

Scanning the eager faces, the first tickle of trepidation went up her spine as she didn't spy the face of her lover. *Surely he's heard of my dilemma by now?* Perhaps he planned a grand rescue at the last moment like the heroes the bards sang of. *How romantic.*

As the last ray of sunlight disappeared and twilight fell, a hush fell over the waiting crowd as Luysa, a smirk of triumph on her face, stepped forward and held up her hands for silence. Firmly spoken words spilled from her lips with a hate and vileness Ysabel could scarcely give credence. *And this is the woman who birthed my sweet Francisco?*

"This most unholy of witches must die. She freely practices her dark craft amongst us."

Heads nodded all around.

Unbelievable. *I practice my arts and use them to cure sick-*

3

ness and aide the healing of infected wounds, Ysabel thought, shaking her head in disbelief. See if she'd help them the next time they came knocking at her door in the middle of the night, the betrayers.

"She uses her magic on our young men, forcing them to do her wicked, unchaste bidding."

Ysabel's brows arched. *Funny, but it was your son who plied me with alcohol the first time he went up my skirts and had his naughty way with me. Of course, I enjoyed it, but still, I never made him do anything.*

"The church says thou shalt not suffer a witch to live. So, I say in the name of God and all that is holy, the witch must die!" Spittle flew as Luysa worked herself into a fever pitch and aimed her last remark toward the back of the crowd. Ysabel followed her gaze and smiled. Francisco had arrived.

I knew he'd come to save me. Take that you crusty, old hag.

Tall, dark and handsome, he looked like something out of a fairy-tale, the type of story her grandmother used to tell her. A true hero, come to save his damsel from the wicked witch. Well in this case, he was saving the witch from the wicked, almost, mother-in-law. He pushed his way to the front of the crowd until he stood before his mother and the stake upon which Ysabel hung. His dark eyes darted to Ysabel's for a moment and a frisson of fear finally tickled down her spine. She didn't see anger in his expression at her situation. No fear at how closely she treaded death's path. In his eyes, she read the truth. And it wasn't pretty.

I'm going to burn, and he's not going to do a damn thing to save me.

Disbelief made her forget the avidly watching crowd.

"Francisco. Tell your mother, I did nothing to bespell you. Tell her of our love for each other." She didn't want to beg, but she couldn't bring herself to believe the dispassionate man in front of her was the same lover who'd murmured such sweet promises.

He didn't reply and at his silence his mother turned to face Ysabel, a look of triumph on her face. "You shall die for your sins, witch." The lit torch was thrust into the ruling harridan's hand and she held it aloft for a moment. "Brujería!" she shouted. "Burn you unholy thing." Then she lowered the flaming brand, and the dry tinder lit with a whoosh.

Panic clawed at Ysabel as the hopelessness of her situation came home. Too late, she struggled in vain at the bindings holding her. But the rope didn't budge. Damn Pedro and his rope tying skill. The crackling sound of the flames grew, aided by the ale Alvaro accidentally spilled on the pyre.

Worse than the view of the spreading fire, was the billowing black smoke and encroaching heat. The first entered her lungs and she coughed as tears streamed from her itching eyes.

Sweat beaded on her face as she worked frantically to free herself, her simple spells and charms of healing no match against her captivity and the element of fire.

With frantic eyes, she scanned the crowd, waiting for someone to step forward and cry foul, to come to her aid, but they watched, some in morbid fascination, some with a sick glee, as the flames grew closer. She caught Francisco's gaze and this time, he didn't turn away. She pled with her eyes for rescue. Acknowledgement. Anything from the man who'd declared he'd do anything for her. Climb the highest mountain. Defy the wishes of his family. Do anything for her love.

Lies. All of it lies, she understood now as he stood there, unflinching while the fire leapt higher, licking at the hems of her skirt, toasting her toes. He showed not a hint of remorse as he watched her burn.

Fury enveloped her, hotter than the flames licking her body. "Bastardo," she spat. "You used me. Betrayed me like a coward. I can't wait to see you in Hell. I'll see all of you in Hell for this." She closed her eyes and began chanting, a dark prayer she'd never thought to use. A last resort her grandmother taught her, but told her to forget. A promise to the Dark Lord – one that wouldn't save her mortal life, but would grant her revenge on those who'd betrayed her. The darkest, most powerful of curses crossed her lips.

As the flames curled around the skin of her feet, burning them and drawing forth screams of agony, she gave her life and soul to the Underlord in return for vengeance. She promised the Devil, whom she worshipped in hiding, anything – her life, her soul, her devotion. He could have it all for a chance to bring Francisco, his mother, and all the sheep-like villagers who rejoiced, into Hell with her. Her cackling laughter at the end of her death spell sounded more like a coughing choke, but thankfully, Lucifer read her intent, and granted her wish. She should have read the fine print.

1

Centuries later...

"Stupid, bloody Devil and his hell-be-damned clauses," Ysabel grumbled under her breath as she stomped to her Lord's office.

Receiving his imperious summons – essentially his voice booming from the walls themselves and ordering her to move her sweet cheeks – she immediately began cursing. Lord of the Underworld or not, the man was truly a pain in her ass. Didn't he know she had better things to do with her time than run when he summoned, like trimming her nails, or washing her hair? Besides, according to the terms of the contract she'd agreed to over five hundred years ago – signed in her still sizzling blood no less – her time as his personal assistant was almost up. Freedom beckoned just around the corner and she couldn't wait, even if she didn't have the slightest clue what she would do with all her upcoming spare time.

Gardening in the Pit wasn't feasible. Joining the general populace made her shudder. What did that leave?

No matter. She'd find a hobby. One definite benefit? Not having to answer the devil's every beck and call. *Just a few more days, then I'm free.*

Of course, Lucifer didn't care if their tenure together was coming to a close. The man got sadistic pleasure out of goading her, reminding her that she wholeheartedly agreed to be his personal slave in exchange for revenge. Thankfully, his idea of chores involved the menial kind; phone answering, filing paperwork, customer – AKA damned souls – relations. In other words, mostly clerical work, a small price to pay when it meant that those who had a direct hand in her burning would be punished eternally for their sin. Vengeance tasted beautifully sweet.

Heels clacking on the slate floor – because Lucifer, stuck in the middle ages, clung like a leech to a dungeon/medieval castle theme – she made her way to the throne room where the Lord of Hell liked to rule his subjects, or, as Ysabel liked to call them, Heaven's leftovers.

When a person died, if they lived an absolutely pure life, free of sin, even the teensy tiniest one, they went to Heaven. Slide across the line into bad, even if you just took the *other* Lord's name in vain once, and you were screwed, doomed to an undying life as a damned soul.

Welcome to Hell, where the living conditions went beyond crowded, the jobs sucked, and the pay sucked even worse. It was like living in, well, Hell.

Forget the ash strewn streets and tenement housing. The inconveniences of the Pit paled beside Lucifer, a true prick of a boss. He brought new meaning to the term sexual harassment. Although, she'd cured him of his ass grabbing habit by wearing a skirt braided with tiny silver slivers... Did she forget to mention they were blessed?

Cost her a fortune to acquire seeing as how some demons had to smuggle it from the mortal side, but worth every damned coin when the Prince of Darkness – dressed in his stupid Darth Vader cape – hopped up and down in his office shaking his hand, bellowing.

The video she'd taken, and threatened to post on Hell-Tube, helped her finagle a private suite in the west wing of the castle. Peace and quiet at la–

"Ysabel!" Lucifer's yodel made her grimace. "I know you're out in that hall, woman. Stop testing my patience and get your ass in here so I can explain before it happens."

Explain what? Waving to his shriveled secretary, she swept past the reception area and pulled open the massive door to his office and stepped in. Her heels tapped on the floor as she headed to her boss, who paced in front of a massive carved desk. It should be noted that the magnificent piece of furniture was carved out of bone, the creature to whom it belonged hopefully extinct, given the ridiculous size of the jaw the artist used. As usual, folders of all thickness and colors covered the desk's gleaming, ivory surface.

Great. More filing. Looks like I'm working late tonight.

The business of selling one's soul boomed, which meant more work and no raise. *I should have joined the minions union.*

"About time you got here," Lucifer said, as he halted his pacing to face her. She paused and waited as he did his usual once over, his eyes lingering on her tits before traveling down. Sure, she could have ruined his enjoyment by wearing something nun-like, but she found more enjoyment in showing him what he'd never have. Besides, Devil or not, a girl liked a man to find her attractive. She cocked a hip and waited for him to finish.

His gaze hit her feet and his brow creased. "Uh-oh. You might want to kick off those expensive pumps of yours."

"Why?" she asked staring down at her shoes. Ridiculously high heeled, and an eye popping purple, green and blue, meant to resemble a peacock's feathers, she didn't care if her toes hurt, or if she didn't exactly have the slim kind of thighs the shoes demanded. She discovered a fetish for shoes in the eighteenth century, probably because she spent most of her mortal life barefoot. Her collection now numbered in the hundreds and the pair she currently wore were fantastic, stolen from the corpse of a favorite movie star – again, an item that cost her a ridiculous sum to smuggle, but so worth it in her mind.

"Don't say I didn't warn you," he muttered enigmatically.

It started with a tickle of her toes that turned into a hot itch. She shifted her weight, wiggling her little piggies. It didn't help. Her feet ignited. Despite her usual cool, Ysabel shrieked, and it wasn't very ladylike. "What the fuck are you doing to my feet?" Forget her feet, the flames licked higher, up her bare legs, snagging her short, white skirt – a color worn to annoy her boss – then, her magenta silk blouse. Engulfed head to toe, a living, screaming torch, the moment brought back the nightmares of the way she'd died.

Dammit! It took hundreds of years of reliving that

awful moment before she eventually prevailed and put her memories of burning at the stake away. It took only seconds of getting torched, once again alive, to bring it all back.

"Goddamn, donkey fucking, bastard, whoring…" The list of words went on and on, because despite her fiery new look, she remained conscious the entire time. More annoying – though her body survived sans blister and flaking skin, the pain was just as excruciating as she remembered.

White foam hit her in the face, shutting her up. The same soothing cool smothered the rest of her body, dousing the flames. It didn't take away the ache in her skin, but at least she wasn't ablaze anymore. She couldn't say as much for her temper. It simmered, held at bay only because she couldn't see the object of her ire and feared opening her mouth and getting a taste of the chemicals used to put her out.

"Hold out your hand," Lucifer said.

She did as told for once and felt a cloth dropped into her palm. Wiping her face first, she opened her eyes and glared at the Lord of the Pit.

For those who'd not met him before – but probably eventually would, because chances were you'd already sinned – the man everyone feared looked like an ordinary business man. Kind of tall at about five eleven or so, with a stocky build and dark hair going silver at the temples. If one ignored the wicked orange fires in his eyes, he would look almost benign. Until he smiled. How he could make something so innocent as the curve of his lips appear so evil, she didn't know, but she practiced, every night in the mirror, to no avail. She just couldn't make her apple cheeks and dimple look grim, no matter how she tried.

"What the fuck just happened?" she asked in a tight voice.

"You were on fire," he calmly replied before turning and heading back to his desk.

Controlling an urge to fling a curse at his back took her a few seconds. Not because holding her temper was the right thing to do but because the jerk possessed a bouncing spellshield on him, kind of like the kids rhyme – 'I'm rubber you're glue, whatever you say, bounces off me and sticks to you.' *Ouch* was all she had to say on that matter.

"Okay, oh king of observation, I was on fire. Care to tell me why?"

Lucifer shuffled some papers on his desk as she stalked toward him – clip, clunk, on uneven heels – as gobs of extinguisher foam fell off her to the floor. Flicking her gaze down, she shrieked.

"I'm naked!"

"Yeah, I noticed. Nice tits by the way. Did I mention you might want to look into getting some flame retardant clothes?"

Eyes narrowed, she shook her finger at him. "You. Explain. Now. And get me some fucking clothes or Lord of Hell or not, I'm going to rip your eyeballs from your head and shove them where the sun never shines."

She knew she'd gone too far when his body began to expand and smoke poured from his ears.

"Enough!" he roared, the force of his yell shaking the room. Dust sifted down. "I might have to put up with this kind of attitude from my daughter, but dammit, you work for me!"

"Not for long," she muttered not in the slightest cowed. Lucifer yelled a lot. Tortured and killed at will too, but, as she'd learned over the years, he respected people with backbone. Of course, he respected it only in private. In public, she smartly bowed and scraped like all his other minions. He did have a reputation to uphold after all. Some lines she knew better than to cross. But alone...she didn't take shit from anyone. Oddly enough, she got the impression he liked her feisty attitude.

"About the termination of your contract – we have a slight problem." He snapped his fingers, and using some kind of magic she had yet to decipher, the burnt remnants of clothing, the foam, everything about her mishap disappeared, including the lingering pain. She dropped into a chair, relieved but not wanting to show it, glad for the simple robe he'd conjured that hid her body. Exhibitionism was for those who went to the gym on a regular basis.

"What problem? We signed a deal, Lucifer. In exchange for my soul and five hundred years of service, you were going to condemn all those who had an active hand in making me burn to an eternity of suffering in Hell. Seems pretty straightforward, and according to my contract, those five hundred years are up next Tuesday."

"Except, we've had a prison breakout."

"And what does a prison breakout have to do with my contract?"

"Hold on to your panties, and I'll show you. Oh wait, you're not wearing a pair anymore." He leered. She growled. He sighed as he muttered, "You are absolutely no fun."

Reaching below his desk, he grabbed something. The object thumped onto his desk, a green folder thick with paper, and labeled, no surprise, with her name. Slave to the big guy didn't mean she'd rolled over and turned into a docile mouse once she got to the Pit. In the circles of Hell, it was every man/woman/demon for themselves. And after the way her lover betrayed her, Ysabel clung to her freedom and status like a pit-bull, cursing with magic anyone who stood in her way. It seemed the Lord had kept tabs on her shenanigans.

Lucifer flipped open her file and pulled out from it, in another feat of magic she hadn't mastered, a yellowed scroll bound in a lock of her hair. He sliced a fingernail across it, splitting the binding and the paper unrolled several feet, revealing line after line of tight handwritten script. He flattened it on his desk, using a pair of paper-weights – the skulls of those who dared defy him – to hold down its corners. Ysabel stood and leaned over to verify it, noting her signature: a giant 'Y' – the only letter she knew how to draw at the time – the blood having dried into an almost black color.

"Why are you showing me this?" she asked.

"Read sub-clause forty-nine, paragraph C, section VII."

Her eyes scanned the document, her lips moving as she read, a skill she'd not owned at the time of signing. She'd had someone impartial brought in to read it for her, a powerful witch by the name of Nefertiti. She'd apprenticed under the sorceress for a time after her arrival, but Nefertiti's brand of magic – sex based orgies for power – wasn't something that appealed.

Oddly enough, though she'd read hundreds of contracts for other souls, this was the first time she'd actually read her own. The more she read, though, the more she wished she'd paid attention at the time instead of being so focused on vengeance. But then again, impartiality was hard to achieve with memories of her skin flaking off and the imagined scent of her own roasted body making her hungry for chicken.

"If I'm reading this right," she said slowly, trying in vain to control her temper, "it says that if within my five hundred years of service, should one of the five I bargained to have cursed and sent to Hell manages to escape, then the terms of my employment are extended until the soul in question is caught."

"Keep reading," he replied. "And keep in mind, this is a standard contract."

Eyes flicking back to the document, she read the rest before grabbing the closest paperweight and throwing it at him. "You jerk! The prison breakout was by one of the souls I had damned to an eternity of suffering, wasn't it? Which means I am going to have to relive the moment of my death, daily, until the soul is caught."

She couldn't help bitching. "This is unfair. Why the hell am I being punished? Your lackeys are the ones who slacked on the job. Punish them."

Lips tight, his eyes glowed in a way that sat her back in her chair, the heaviness of his power pressing on her. "Oh, they are reaping the rewards of my displeasure, fear not. But, enough about them. We need to fix this. If we're to be free of each other in a week, then you need to get moving."

"Me?"

"Yes you. You just read the contract. The same way you cursed those people and dragged their souls to me upon their untimely deaths, now that they're missing, it's up to you to bring those souls back."

"Souls? Are you telling me you lost more than one?"

The Lord of The Pit actually looked sheepish. "What can I say? Good minions are hard to come by. Ever since the problems of the past few years with Lilith and that revolt, well, the demon army still hasn't recovered its numbers yet. And the mortal realm doesn't make soldiers like they used to. Ah for the days when Vikings roamed the seas and pillaged whole villages. I even miss those feisty Spartans. Now those were some souls with substance and skills."

Ysabel slapped a hand over her forehead. "I don't believe this. I'm the one scheduled to catch fire every day until I fix your mistake and you're giving me excuses and reminiscing? That's fucking priceless. And just how am I supposed to find and catch the escapees?"

"There are five of them and if you tag them with this pin," Lucifer slid a metallic box in her direction. "Then they'll be taken straight to processing."

"Yay, so I've got an easy way to get them back," she drawled sarcastically. "You still haven't mentioned exactly how I'm supposed to find them."

"Don't you have some witchy method for tracking people?" he asked. "I had the guards collect some of their skin. Of course, I don't know whose is whose given we wiped it off the lashes after they disappeared, but DNA is still the best identifier." He smiled.

She glared.

A big sigh left him. "What do you want from me? This

wasn't done on purpose, I assure you. I'd like nothing more than for you and I to be rid of each other. But even *I* can't break the contract."

In that respect, he told the truth. If a person swore an oath in Hell and then signed it with blood, it couldn't be broken until the terms of the contact were complete. No one knew why, not even Lucifer. It seemed there were more powers out there than just those of Heaven and Hell.

"And if I say screw you and the souls stay free?"

"You will burn, every single day, at the time of your death, one extra minute per day, the pain growing more and more excruciating with each day that passes."

"Is that all?" she queried sarcastically.

"No." He bore a serious expression which frightened her more than his words. Lucifer always spoke with a smile – evil smile, naughty grin, provocative leer. She didn't think she wanted to hear what came next.

"If you don't bring those souls back, you'll go mad. Lose your mind. Go completely off your rocker. It's not pretty. I've seen it before. It happened to Bambi's mother. I had to throw her in the abyss myself. You've met my eldest daughter, Bambi haven't you? Won Biggest Slut in the world five years running, you know?"

Yes, she knew. Everyone knew Bambi. The males all wanted a turn with Hell's most famous succubus, while the females did their best to keep their men away. While the reminder of Bambi's skills in the boudoir made her shudder, his mention of the abyss gave her a chill.

What few people earth-side knew was Hell didn't mean the end of a person's life, for damned souls at any rate. Once a mortal sinned and died, changing their residential address to Hell, they could technically live forever. Sounded like a great prize, right? Not really. Eking out any kind of existence in the Underworld took a lot of work. Housing sucked. Jobs rated even worse. And forget killing to free up some room or take someone's spot.

Mortal wounds, while painful to the recipient, couldn't kill the damned. Nor decapitation or any other torture devised – a great trick that Lucifer used to punish the truly wicked. Only one thing alone could put a spirit to rest. The abyss.

At the very center of Hell, nestled within the spirals of the nine circles, the great gaping hole was where a soul went when they were conquered their fear of the final death. When the tedium of day to day living in the Pit finally got to them, or they'd atoned for their sins, they could make the pilgrimage to the abyss, toss themselves in and, eventually, end up reborn again.

Or so the rumors stated.

Witches bound to Lucifer before death, didn't quite own their souls – and no one knew where he hid them – so uncertainty prevailed, along with numerous debates, on what would happen to them if they jumped in. She'd rather not find out. But if the pain became too much, would she still feel the same?

Something of her thought process must have been reflected in her face because Lucifer gave her a paternal smile meant to reassure. "I'm sure you'll manage to capture them before you go nuts. And if not, I know a place that sells straitjackets for cheap."

She covered her face with a moaned, "Why me?"

"Oh no. Cut the girly crap right now. You know I hate it when women get sentimental. So let's stick to business.

You need to catch those souls or you're going to be a very unhappy witch, which in turns means I'll have to listen to you bitching and moaning because you'll still be working for me. If I can't get rid of you, it will cut into my golf game. With Mother Earth visiting her tree groves for her spring inspection, I only have a limited amount of time to practice before she gets back and insists we work on our relationship. Blech." He made a face.

"This is impossible, you know," she said. "I don't know how you expect me to find that many souls by myself. Are you sure the burning thing will be that bad?" Actually, even the mention of it brought a shudder. And it was supposed to get worse? She needed to find those souls pronto.

"I'd love to help you, but I'm understaffed." His big, white toothed grin screamed, 'I'm lying.'

"I've got a video of you doing the Macarena."

He scowled. "I hate you. You're just like another pesky daughter to me. Fine. Twist my arm. I'll give you a tracker to use. But it will cost you."

She arched a brow.

"Or not. Now get out."

"In a second. Hold on to your storm trooper boots. This burning thing – how long will it last each day?"

"At precisely eight forty-seven p.m. each day, you will catch on fire."

"In case you hadn't noticed, it's two forty seven p.m. or was when I walked in."

"We're on Eastern Standard time here. Not Central European. Now, as I was saying, each day, at the time of your death, you will catch fire, reliving the moment. The burning will last one minute the first day, then increase each day by another minute. Anything you wear will burn to a crisp. The good news, though, is that your hair and body will remain untouched, you'll just feel it. And once the flames extinguish, it might take a few minutes for the pain to fade."

"That sounds lovely," she replied, her face twisting in a grimace. "Anything else I should know?"

"Well, it goes without saying that if during your quest to find the escapees you end up on the mortal plane, stay out of sight. Human authorities might get a little weirded out if you catch fire and walk away."

"I guess I'm shopping for practical clothes," she muttered with a moue of distaste. She rose from the chair. "Send your tracker to my place in about six hours. I want to get started on this right away."

"Good luck," the devil said quietly, and if she didn't know better, she'd have said he sounded sincere.

Nah. Probably more like morose that they might get stuck with each other past the expiry date on her contract.

Not if she could help it.

But first she needed to go shopping for flame retardant clothes that would go well with soul hunting. Lucky for her, she'd swiped her boss's credit card, so the sky was the limit. And she had a whole spare bedroom that could handle the extra garments.

2

WHISTLING, Remy strolled to Lucifer's office. Getting called to see his boss could mean only one of two things. Either he was in trouble – which considering he'd not slept with any of his Lord's daughters seemed unlikely – or he was getting a special assignment. The latter would totally work right now given he'd just ended a few relationships, mostly because they found out about each other.

Females – they could act so irrational when it came to sharing him. Didn't they know he had enough stamina to please them all? Yeah, that was one line he'd have to strike from his repartee list. Not one of them liked it, no matter how engaging his smile as he said it. As his one lady friend – a hot blonde demon who could suck a golf ball through a garden hose – dumped his clothing out of the window onto a pile of refuse, he came to the realization that perhaps the time had come for him to concentrate on one lady at a time. The thrill of a variety of pussy, once all he could think about, had worn off. *Surprising, I know.* He never thought that would happen. But truly, he'd come to realize, all females were the same in the end; same to please, same to scream, same to drive him nuts. So why continue with the headache that came with juggling several?

Why, he might even settle down with one lucky female and pop out a demon spawn or two. He snorted at the thought. *Let's not get crazy here.* Deciding to bed one female at a time was one thing, at one hundred and four years, he was still kind of young to be thinking of starting a family, even if a lot of his buddies seemed to have jumped into that particular hot pan. And happily, too.

Remy couldn't imagine wanting to consign himself to a life with one female, because while fooling around as a single man with more than one lucky lady was accepted, once a demon decided to start a family and bind himself into their version of matrimony, cheating was out of the question – if he wanted to keep his balls intact. Demon wives took a strict stance on cheating, and abetted by other wives, and even mothers, made sure the males didn't cross that line – or else. Knowing that, it was a wonder to him any man every chose to mate with one female.

It's probably some kind of insanity that grips them when they get to a certain age. Or a spell. Lucky for him, Remy had a resistance to magical attacks on his person.

Arriving at the vestibule for Lucifer's secretary, he gave his name to the shriveled crone manning the desk. Ugly, old, misshapen, and possessed of an odd smell, rumor said Gaia herself chose the woman for the position after Lucifer's last secretary came to work one too many times in sheer blouses, braless of course. Last he heard, the blonde bimbo, who'd given more than one demon in the ranks a wild ride, was on latrine duty for the women's prison. It didn't pay to piss off his Lord's on again, off again, girlfriend.

Hey, I wonder if I can get any clues on whether he's going to pop the question to his old lady. A great amount of betting currently existed in all the nine circles based on when their Lord would finally get the guts to ask Gaia to marry him. Remy had several paychecks riding on his date of August thirteenth, two thousand thirteen, a date that fast approached and with nary a jeweler claiming credit for an engagement ring design at this point.

While he waited to be admitted to his Lord's inner sanctum, he looked around, noting the closed door with the gold embossed title, 'Satan's Assistant,' and etched underneath, 'Go Away.' With that kind of welcoming attitude, he counted himself lucky he'd never come face to face with his boss's damned soul relations manager. He'd heard the terms harridan, witch, bitch, along with a whole list of other not-very-nice adjectives used to describe the zealous female in charge of keeping Hell's contracts in order. But, the woman who scared the crap out of even the hardest criminals in the pit dealt with damned souls only, not demons, so he thankfully never had to meet with the obviously ugly shrew with the not-so-shining personality everyone spoke of.

Striding into his Lord's office, he snapped to attention. "First class demon, Remy Crafir, reporting as ordered, sir."

"At ease, soldier."

As if, Remy almost said aloud. Only demons with a death wish let themselves relax in the big man's presence.

His boss, dressed in his usual business attire, drummed his fingers on his massive desk.

"You've been working for me how long now, soldier?"

Odd question since Lucifer already knew. "Since the eighteenth year of my birth, sir."

"And you are now…"

"One hundred and four, sir." *And in my prime,* he thought puffing out his chest lest his boss think he was getting old.

"You've seen a lot of danger I would imagine during your tenure."

"Sir?"

"Just talking to myself. I know what you've accomplished, some of it at my direct behest. Your commanding officers have only positive things to say about your service. Blood-thirsty. Single minded. Thorough. And a panty-dropper among the ladies."

Who could resist a grin at having the Lord of the Pit shoot a conspiratorial smile at the last bit?

"Ever think of settling down, soldier?" Lucifer leaned forward and steepled his fingers on his desktop.

"Excuse me, sir?"

"Settle down with a female. Make some babies. Your mother was about your age when she had you."

"Sir, with all due respect, she is a little crazy. And her decision to have a human as my father wasn't exactly a sound one."

"Got a problem with only being a half demon, soldier? My son is a half demon."

Oh shit, he'd insulted his Lord. "I am quite glad to be a half demon?" He said it questioningly, and when his boss didn't decapitate him, but kept staring, waiting for more,

24

he thought quickly. "There're a lot of advantages to my half demon status. I, um, can use my magic on the mortal plane." At Lucifer's encouraging nod, he kept going. "I am long lived like a full demon." But thinner skinned, so more prone to injury, which sucked. "I heal quickly. I'm strong. I'm impervious to fire." A trait he got from his mother, an almost pure blooded fire demon.

"And you aren't ugly like most of my pure bred demons. It's all right, soldier, you can say it. Demons mixing with demons doesn't always produce the prettiest babies."

"If you say so, sir."

"I do and if the reports I've read about you are true, I'd say the ladies agree." Lucifer winked, and Remy grinned. "But, now on to the real reason I called you here. I have a special assignment for you, soldier."

"Whatever my lord wishes."

"Of course. But, still, I feel I should warn you, it's going to be a rough one. Worse than all the other missions I've sent you on. You need to fetch five souls back from the mortal realm."

Piece of cake. He could do that with one arm tied behind his back. "Consider it done, sir."

"Hold on, it's not going to be that easy. Unfortunately, the souls in question are bound by a curse, so while you can help hunt them, someone else needs to send them back to Hell. You are to aid her."

"Her? I am to partner with a female?" The ranks of Lucifer's armies had a few female demons, although no one would dare call them girly to their face. Someone like that wouldn't need his help though. So who did Lucifer think to pair him with?

"Yes a woman. An annoying shrew who will possibly drive you insane."

"She can try." After all, if his nut job of a mother didn't succeed, he doubted anyone could.

"Oh, she will, soldier. I thought I'd give you fair warning, not my usual thing. I prefer to watch the sparks fly, but this is one time, I'd like one of my bound servants to succeed. And quickly, too."

"When do I start?"

"Eager to meet your doom? I like that in a man."

"No time like the present, sir."

"Excellent. You start now. Here's her address. Oh and one last piece of advice. Wear a cup and keep your hands to yourself."

"Why? Is she a hottie?" He should be so lucky, a mission and new pussy, all in one day.

"She's a five hundred year old witch who has a hate on for men."

Great, stuck with a hag. Ah well, he'd still have fun since it seemed more than likely he'd get to roam the mortal plane. Most escaped souls tended to make their way to the surface as soon as possible. No reason he couldn't mix in a bit of pleasure while he worked.

"Consider it done."

"Good luck," Lucifer said soberly. "You'll need it."

Dismissed, Remy snapped a salute before turning on a heel and exiting his boss's office. Whistling the refrain to a dirty melody, he strode through his Lord's castle wondering who this servant was that needed his aid and managed to finagle a coveted spot in the boss man's house. Usually, Remy would assume the witch slept with Lucifer, but given his boss's description and warning, it sounded more like she was a pain in the ass, which was fine. Remy had plenty of experience with ass, taking that was, not being.

Knocking on a massive carved door minutes later, the sigils on it shouting to those literate enough to 'Stay away or else!' he received a nice surprise when the door swung open. *Well, hello there.*

Reaching only his shoulder, with a wild mop of black hair, bright brown eyes and a rounded body made for worship – by his tongue – Remy wondered if he could convince the servant girl to come around the corner with him for a quickie before he met with this Ysabel person. Then she opened her luscious mouth.

"If you're done gawking, you might want to step back before I smash your nose with the door when I shut it."

Someone got up without sex today. He could fix that. "Hello beautiful, I actually have business with the occupant of this suite. I'm here to meet with Ysabel, the witch."

"Really." Her tone said what she thought of his claim and her brown gaze looked him up and down, then dismissed him. "I don't think so."

The door slammed shut in his face.

What. The. Fuck.

Remy pounded on the door. It immediately opened. The ebony haired vixen, her arms crossed under her bountiful tits, smirked. "Back already. What's wrong? Did I hurt your feelings?"

"Listen woman, I don't know what crawled up your ass and turned you into an uptight bitch, but I'm here to see Ysabel, so get the fuck out of my way before I put you over my knee and –"

"And what? Spank me?" Her eyes actually sparked with

challenge, the minx. "I'd like to see you try. But, before you do, just so you know, my name is Ysabel. The witch."

Aaaaah, shit. Never one to admit defeat, he let a slow simmering smile spread across his face. It worked on demonesses, damned souls, human women, and even gay men, but apparently, it had no effect on scowling witches. Too bad. "It's your lucky day. Lucifer has informed me that you're my next assignment."

"Not by choice. And what are you supposed to do exactly? I need a tracker, not a gigolo. What happened? Did your gig as a pole dancer not work out? Equipment too small?" She dropped her gaze to his groin and sneered.

A sudden, irrational urge possessed him to drop his pants, flip her over and show her there was nothing wrong with the size of his cock. He abstained, but couldn't prevent himself from taunting her, eyeing her up and down in the same dismissive manner. "Anytime you want to measure my dick, you let me know. Naked."

"Pig."

"No, demon. Really, get your terminology straight, would you? After Lucifer's warning, I expected someone older and badder."

To his credit he didn't drop to the ground, but the pain in his balls did require he bend over to cup them gently which in turn meant he got the door in the face. Again. And that was the last straw.

Ysabel stomped away from her door, cussing Lucifer and his perpetual jokes. Sending a half dressed, muscle bound, half demon with the face of an Adonis to help her indeed. She needed brains not –

Bang!

Her door, her spelled door she might add, splintered into shards as he stalked into her place, eyes glowing red, muscles bunched, lips taut with anger. Women would have swooned at his virile appearance. She held her ground – but couldn't help a tingle. He truly was good looking, and even though she knew good looking men were the scum of the earth – er, Hell, that was – even she could admit that if she were to choose a male to scratch a sexual itch, she'd want his number.

It pissed her off. She didn't get involved with men. Demons. Or anything at all for that matter. Tucking away her body's unexpected interest, she pursed her lips at the object of her irritation.

Since he didn't like *no* for an answer, she switched tactics. There was more than one way to make a male run, and when the bitchy method didn't work…

She clutched her chest and widened her eyes. "You, you broke my door."

"Yes I did," he snarled. "And kick me again in the balls and I'll–"

She squeezed one fake tear. "Please don't hurt me. I'm sorry. It's just, a big bad demon shows up at my door and you took me by surprise. And Lucifer is sending me on this scary quest…" She sniffed.

And he gobbled it up, hook, line, and sinker. The tension in his body eased, he lost the angry glow in his eyes, and he even tendered a masculine smile that made her sex tingle in a most annoying way. It was his drawled,

"Sorry, baby, didn't mean to scare you," that pushed her over the edge.

It emerged as a choked sound at first, but turned into full blown laughter. She clutched her stomach as she laughed, the best one she'd had in what seemed like ages. And it just got better the more he scowled.

"Oh," she gasped in between giggles. "I can't believe you fell for that. Did you really think a witch of my caliber and age would really be so fucking weak?"

"I was being a gentleman."

She snorted. "Ah yes, because gentlemen show up at the door all the time expecting the help to drop their panties. And when refused turn into dinks."

"Dinks? Wow, little witch, get with the times. It's dick. In my case, you could even say big dick."

"Careful, demon. I've shrunken heads bigger than yours." Her pointed stare at the stop below his belt buckle had him growling.

"Witch, you are testing my patience."

"Then leave."

"I can't. My Lord Lucifer has ordered me to help you, and by all that is evil in this place, I shall, whether you like it or not. Keep denying me, and I'll have you screaming with your panties around your ankles."

"Ooh, what a big demon, resorting to rape when he doesn't get his way."

"Ha. I don't need to force a woman. I was talking about spanking you over my knee, the proper punishment for a woman who's acting like a brat. Although, if you'd prefer to scream because I'm making you cum, just say so. I'm sure you could convince me to hold off on punishment. Especially if you got on your knees, naked."

"You are unbelievable." In more than one way. It seemed his good looks came with a set of balls that didn't let him back down even faced with a woman who could string words into a sentence. *Bet he doesn't come across a girl with a brain too often.* In his case, he probably judged their IQ on the size of their melons.

And what a crude mouth he owned. Who said ridiculous things like 'I'll have you screaming with your panties around your ankles'? Even scarier, what stupid woman fell for his corny pickup lines? *Not me.*

"I hear that a lot from my lady friends," he agreed with a wink.

"And I'll bet you have plenty as a pole dancer. Like I said before, I need a tracker, not a Chippendale Demon. So why don't you run off and hand-wash your gold lame g-string while I get on with the job. Don't worry. I won't tell Lucifer on you. He might try to stick me with someone worse, like your even more annoying twin brother."

"No need to wash anything, little witch, I prefer to go commando. And while I am flattered you think me attractive enough to dance for a living, the truth is I am a tracker and fighter – a damned good one too. So, if you want to be rid of me, the fastest way is for us to get started."

She sighed. "You're not going to leave are you?"

"Not a chance. So, suck it up buttercup."

"I am really starting to dislike you."

"You know what they say: dislike is akin to lust."

"That's not the expression."

"It is in my world. You wouldn't be the first one to tell me you hate me only to rip my clothes off and ride me

31

like a wild cowgirl."

"I will not! When we're done, I'm going to carve your balls and –"

"Touch my balls with harmful intent and you'll be tea-bagging them," he warned.

Stymied she had to ask. "What the hell does that mean?"

An enigmatic smile graced his lips. It made more than her sex tingle, her tits joined the game too, hardening into points "Why don't you touch them and find out?"

"Pig."

"I prefer the term rutting beast. Now, if we're done. Do you know who the missing targets are?"

Shooting him a glare, a dirty look he pretended to not notice, she pointed to the folders Lucifer had delivered to her home. Sinking onto her couch, the half demon took up a lot of space. She studied him as he grabbed the first file and read. She bit her tongue before she asked him if he needed help with the big words. Why she wanted to antagonize him, she didn't understand, but she couldn't deny she enjoyed their verbal sparring. Most males resorted to brute force when faced with her admittedly viperish tongue. He disarmed her with words and innuendo. More alarming, it partially worked.

I'll bet you it wouldn't have, though, if he'd proven butt ugly.

Tall, way taller than her five foot five frame, his body bulged with muscles covered in tanned skin. He possessed layered brown hair with gold highlights, vivid turquoise eyes and chiseled features, including a strong straight nose – surprising because with a taunting mouth like his she expected he'd gotten it broken more than once in his life – a square chin, and wickedly full lips that now quirked into a grin.

"Enjoying the view?" he taunted.

"Deciding what part to carve off your body first," she replied. "Do you have a name by the way? Or should I just refer to you as 'that asshole'?"

"You can call me Remy, but, when I get your thighs around my neck, feel free to call me God. It totally pisses Lucifer's brother off, which means brownie points for me."

A blush tried to heat its way into her cheeks at the mental image he provoked. His nude body, thrusting into her… Damn, she needed a cold shower and a few minutes alone with her vibrator. "Are you always this crass?"

"What can I say?" he replied spreading his hands wide with a beaming smile. "You bring out the best in me. Although, I'd prefer to sink my best into you," he winked.

She gaped, more because she lost the power of speech as a surge of lust raced through her. Totally unacceptable.

As she stomped off to the kitchen for something to drink – preferably ice cold so she could cool the fever trying to overtake her body – she wondered at his game. All demons played one.

Some thrived on violence and mayhem. Some liked to lie and watch the resulting chaos play itself out. Others liked to burn things. Kill things. Hunt. Fuck. If it pleased Lucifer, they did it. If it fed the dark part they all owned, they craved it. Demons weren't human and thus didn't possess the same morals and restraints that conditioned mortal behavior. Even half ones, like Remy, who appeared human, contained a kernel of bad. And because of it, they just couldn't help themselves.

That wasn't to say all demons were evil, war mongering psychopaths – even if many were. Despite their love of mischief and mayhem, the tricky beasts could also love, and prove themselves trustworthy. But most reserved that aspect of their personality for others of their kind. They had little time for the damned, who lived out their pitiful lives in the circles of Hell. They enjoyed humans that still lived on the surface as one would a pet, a fragile pet that was short lived. As for witches, the undead and other types of entities roaming the dimension of Heaven, Hell and the void in between? They mixed, just not often, and when it did occur it was mostly about fulfilling a sexual need.

A need she'd ignored for five hundred years, satisfying herself when necessary, alone. Ysabel preferred solitude. Even with her own kind, she avoided interaction, disliking on sight most warlocks with their pompous airs. She didn't trust the other sorceresses, who especially liked to guard their secrets and power, even if they all worked for the Lord of the Pit. If she could truly call one person her friend it would be Nefertiti, the most powerful witch she knew, one with a bevy of lovers. While Ysabel found her brand of sexual based magic not to her taste, she enjoyed the nuggets of wisdom – and even more guiltily, the ribald jests –Nefertiti chose to impart.

Despite her less than inviting personality, Ysabel inad-vertently had a few other friends; a psycho – with anger issues that could only be resolved by killing things; a lamia – who went through men as quick as she shed skin; even a vampiress – who was allergic to human blood. Oh, she shouldn't forget Muriel, Lucifer's daughter, who wouldn't go away no matter how many times she slammed the door in her face. Over time, though, she grew quite fond of her. Who wouldn't when the girl possessed an uncanny ability to drive the Lord to the brink of insanity where he yanked his hair and snorted fire? Muriel was quite the character, and now that she'd settled down, Ysabel at times envied her the home life she'd found with her fallen angel, gorgeous kitty, and undead hunk. While a threesome was not her style – heck, she didn't even care for a onesome – she couldn't deny the longing to find the same kind of happiness as her friend. The bitch.

"Hell to witch. Hell to witch. Do you read me?"

Snapping back to attention she found the hot and sexy demon waving his hand in front of her.

"What?"

"I hate to break your obvious fantasy of me doing delightful things to your body, but, I think I know where to find the first guy."

"Where?"

"According to his file, he's been having mirror sex with a human on the mortal side who's been summoning him. Wanna bet he's gone to get himself a piece of ass?"

Having not read the files, her time since her meeting with Lucifer spent between shopping for clothes that wouldn't ignite and cursing him out, she could only trust – *gag* – the demon's assessment. If he ended up wrong, then she could always cast a location spell using some of the blood they'd scraped off the lash used to punish the damned villagers.

"Can you call a doorway to our target location?"

A scowl didn't make him look any less attractive, the jerk. "No. I didn't get the right half of demon magic for that. We'll have to go through one of the permanent doors."

"I'll get my broom."

"Excuse me?"

She smirked. "Broom, as in transportation."

"What's wrong with stealing a car?"

"A broom is faster because we can fly straight to our target address from the nearest portal and avoid traffic." Batting her lashes at him, she smiled tauntingly. "Don't tell me the big, bad demon is scared of riding a broom? Don't worry, my passengers don't fall off. Often."

With a swish of her hips, she walked away stifling a giggle at his pained expression reflected in a mirror. *Finally, a point for the witch.* She should have known he'd get her back.

3

THE SLENDER POLE of her broom whipped through the seam of his thighs, emerging from him like a three foot long, wooden dick. Grabbing a hold of it, he thrust his hips forward and with a grin said, "Screw Pinocchio's nose. Now this is what I call wood."

"Is everything about sex with you?"

"No. I also enjoy conversing about cunnilingus, masturbation, and the state of Hell's eco system." She blinked and he fought not to chuckle. "What? Don't' tell me you've not heard about the overpopulation of our Pit leading to an increase in methane gases which is impeding the natural fabrication of sulfur."

"Unbelievable," she muttered as she jammed flight goggles onto her head. Not her best look facially, but the rest of her…Tasty!

Wearing skin tight, black pants, that hugged an exquisitely round butt, a black turtleneck and knee high boots, she looked good enough to eat. Or fuck. He wouldn't quibble.

Grabbing the rod, which made him emit a groaned, "Yes, baby, that's it. Pull it," his partner for the job, straddled the spot in front of him.

"Hold on tight," she warned.

Hmm, now that sounded more like it. He wrapped his arms around her waist, held her snugger than necessary, and inched up until his groin pressed against her backside.

"Comfortable?" she asked with a wiggle. Before he could answer, she yanked the broom up, squishing his balls in a most uncomfortable manner.

Why the hell am I doing this again? Oh yeah, because a witch with the naughtiest smirk and taunting attitude dared him. Fuck. The things he did for his job. Okay, that was a lie. He did this just to prove a point. He wasn't scared of–

"Crazy fucking witch!" he shouted as the broom shot straight up and he held on for dear life while fighting the pain in his nuts as they got royally squashed by the several G's now powering the broom.

Her answer to his bellow of annoyance?

"Wheeee!"

And how was a demon supposed to stay pissed – even with throbbing balls – when she showed such delight in soaring through the night sky, her round bottom pressed into his crotch, her body a perfect fit for his arms? He couldn't. A smile crossed his lips. Two could play the game of 'Bet I can annoy you more.'

Hunching his head, his lips found the shell of her ear. "Need directions?" He blew softly at the end of his query and didn't miss the shiver that went through her.

"I've got it programmed in the broom's GPS."

The answer threw him for a loop. In his mind, technology and brooms just didn't mix. But, back to her reaction at his proximity. He whispered again as his arm inched up to brush the underside of her breasts, a gentle nudge. "So why a broom? Wouldn't a carpet be more comfortable? We could have *stretched* out."

"Actually, armchairs make the comfiest ride, but brooms are the easiest to control for some reason. And since Harry Potter, they've made a major comeback. Besides, I like going back to my roots."

"When were you born? The dark ages?"

"I'm almost five hundred and twenty years old, so yes, the dark ages would be about right."

"That's right. You're a cougar!" he exclaimed. "I forgot. That is so fucking hot."

"I am not old! I don't look a day older than twenty two which was my age when I died."

Yeah, he noticed she sported the body of a nubile woman in her prime. "But inside, you're a Mrs. Robinson with centuries of experience to boast. Like I said, fucking hot."

"You're a freak."

"Nope, just totally turned on. Ever make out on a broom?" He let go of her waist to cup her tits, stroking thumbs over peaks already straining through the fabric of her top.

She squeaked. The broom bucked. He clung to her with one arm, but continued to let his other hand play with her breast.

"Stop that." The voice said no, but the breathiness of it and the way her bottom pressed against his hard cock said yes.

"Would you prefer I did this instead?" He let his hand move lower, cupping her mound through her pants. The heat almost burned his fingers. A moment, that was all he had to enjoy the humid warmth between her legs before she flipped the broom upside down and shook it. Still, he would have stayed on if she hadn't muttered, "Electrificar." A zing went through his arm rendering it numb and he ended up losing his grip and plummeting.

Good for him, she'd already begun their descent, so he didn't have far to go. Bad for him, he landed in a swimming pool, which considering he wore leather, led to a cold experience he wouldn't recommend, especially since with all that weight, he sank.

YSABEL PROBABLY SHOULDN'T HAVE GIGGLED AS HE PULLED himself from the pool, water streaming from him in thick rivulets. But really, what did he expect? Groping her while she drove, making her all hot and distracted. The jerk. He should count himself lucky. Most guys would have ended up splattered on the sidewalk. Maybe she didn't hate him after all.

Hair plastered to his skull, dripping like a big sea monster, he glowered at her. "You are an evil witch."

Fluffing her hair she smiled. "Why thank you. I try my best."

Keeping an eye on him for violence, because demons liked to retaliate, she instead gaped as he peeled his leather vest off, and then his shirt. Cool spring night her ass, someone give her a fan because it was hot. Knowing he bore a ton of muscle just didn't prepare a girl for the in the flesh reality of it. She blinked. Swallowed. Clenched her thighs tight, but the fire he'd started while fondling her on the broom just keep burning, hotter and hotter.

"Should I keep going?" he asked with a grin, his hands on the buckle to his leather pants.

"We have a job to do," she mumbled, whirling and stalking toward the condominium where their target hid. And the job didn't include Remy working her over with his tongue, hands and dick. Even if he would agree in a heartbeat and make it feel so fucking good.

I don't sleep with demons. Or men. Or anyone. Don't trust. Because, as she well knew, lovers could betray.

Stomping away, she kept reminding herself of that fact, almost muttered it under her breath as a protective mantra when he caught up to her, his looming, silent presence not something she seemed able to ignore. Not wanting to cart their transportation around, she stashed her broom behind a potted plant by the door. She expected Remy to follow suit with his wet clothes, but when she turned around, she found him dressed again, a hint of steam rising from his clothes.

"Figures you'd be a fire demon."

"It's what makes me so hot." He arched a brow and she snorted.

"Idiot."

A zap from her finger with a muttered word that meant *open* in Spanish, and they were in the building. He crowded her in the elevator and short of staring at the climbing numbers, which screamed cowardice, she couldn't avoid him. She met his amused gaze.

"Why are you smiling?" she asked.

"Thanks for the swim. I needed that. Nothing worse than a major hard on right before a mission."

"Do you ever temper your tongue?" She forced herself not to peek lower than his chin.

"Nope. I just let it do what it wants, and might I say, it does *wicked* things."

"You're impossible."

"No, totally possible, and unforgettable."

"Would you get your mind out of your pants for a second and concentrate on the mission. What's the plan?"

Leaning against the elevator wall, he rolled his wide shoulders in a shrug. "Kick the door in. Tackle the escaped soul. Pin him down while you tag him and send him back to Hell."

"Um, ever heard of subtlety? What if he's not there? What if he's expected later? What if there's an army of fucking U.S. soldiers with guns inside?"

He rolled his eyes. "Fine. I won't kick down the door. What's your plan?"

What did hers consist of? "We'll knock first."

"And?"

"I'll ask if Pedro is there."

"Really? Because I'm sure this girl isn't going to think it's weird that some strange chick is showing up at her door at eleven o'clock at night looking for the ghost she's been conjuring at night for mirror sex."

The frown she bestowed upon him just made him smile. "I've got a new plan," he announced.

"Does it involve kicking down the door again?"

"Nope."

"Are you going to set up a pole and dazzle her with your dancing skills?"

"Nope, but I like the way you mind works. Here's my idea: you knock on the door and do your thing; talk, lull her into a false sense of security, pump her info, pull out her fingernails one by one. Whatever works for you. While you keep her occupied, I'll slip into her place from the balcony."

"How are you going to get to her balcony?"

"Leave that to me."

"That's what I'm afraid of," she muttered.

The smile on his full lips got wider. "Don't worry, my sexy cougar. We'll catch the prick and send him back to Hell. Then you can thank me. Preferably naked. On your knees or back. I'm not picky."

Yeah, he totally deserved the punch in the gut that time. Of course, it hurt her fist more than him seeing as how he was made of granite. The elevator dinged, and, shooting him a dirty look while massaging her knuckles, she exited. He didn't.

"Aren't you coming?"

"I hope to later."

She growled.

He grinned. "You know that look is sexy right?" He laughed at her scowl. "Lighten up, little witch. Just give me five minutes before you knock. You do your thing. I'll do mine and we'll be out of here in no time."

"Why don't I believe that," she grumbled.

The elevator doors slid shut leaving her alone. Oddly, despite only meeting him today she kind of missed him. Demon, pain in the ass or not, he somehow made her feel alive when he was around. *Too alive*, she amended wryly, her body still tingling from his touch and nearness. Why him, and why now?

She'd spent five hundred years easily avoiding males. Not desiring or needing one at all. Then, the most vulgar – good looking – annoying – with a wicked body – demon showed up, and suddenly she wanted to strip naked and dance around him like she'd not had an urge to since the last Beltane she celebrated while still alive.

Jerk.

There would be no naked dancing around or on his pole. Nor any tonguing or other things he'd enjoy too much. Never mind she'd enjoy them too. The man was a womanizing pig. Worse even than Francisco, because Remy didn't even bother to hide it.

It's men like him that make me glad I've sworn off relationships. And no, she didn't care to dwell on the fact the nights were lonely, her dildo not cuddly, and her life boring. She would not go through the pain and heartache that came from a lover's betrayal again.

Not having a watch, she didn't really know how much time went by since she and Remy parted ways. She tapped her foot, paced up the hall and peeked around the corner, waited until her patience ran out, then approached the door of her target.

Three quick raps and she stood back, trying to appear benign. The door crept open and a wary eye, lined in dark kohl, peered out.

"What do you want?" the girl asked suspiciously.

"I was looking for Pedro. I heard he made it out of that awful prison and I wanted to congratulate him." Ysabel pasted on a fake smile.

The orb peering at her narrowed. "How do you know about Pedro?"

"We met through our mirror talks, well, more like

mirror sex." Ysabel forced out a false giggle. "That man sure has a way with words. Especially dirty ones. He told me about you. Said you were one hot conjurer. He also told me when he got out, we should all hook up together, if you know what I mean." Ysabel winked and licked her lips.

The door partially closed but only so the woman on the other side could remove the chain with a rattle. The portal swung open and Ysabel walked into a psychedelic acid trip. Seriously, the tie-die murals, eye-popping cushions on the couch, everything screamed welcome to the seventies – an era she'd experienced second hand on television.

The owner of the place appeared a throwback to the hippy days as well, with her long straight brown hair, flowing patterned skirt and the jangling hoops covering her arms. Ysabel didn't peruse her for long. The human didn't interest her. Turning away, she surveyed the apartment, looking for signs of Pedro.

In his late twenties when she collected his soul, after killing him with a garrote, Pedro was a true asshole. Married to a meek woman, he cheated with anything willing to spread its legs. Some said even the farm animals weren't safe from his advances. He was one of the men who came to fetch her for the pyre. He took great delight in groping her as he carried her to her punishment. Leered as he slid a hand up her skirt under the pretext of looking for a weapon. Whispered disgusting things while he tied the rope. The pervert even sported a hard on as she burned, watching in slack jawed excitement.

He totally deserved what I gave him. Eternal torment.

But, she didn't think he agreed judging by the angry

45

countenance he presented when he strode from the bedroom clad only in a pair of boxer shorts. Not exactly a good look for the barrel chested soul with way too much shag carpeting coating his skin. Hair removal companies would have made a fortune off him.

"Fucking witch! You should have stayed in Hell where you belong."

"I belong? I'm not the sick puppy giving the sheep venereal infections and burning people at the stake."

"Jealous because I wouldn't give you a taste?" he taunted with a grab of his groin.

The gagging wasn't faked. "I think I might never eat again. But enough of your grossness, say goodbye to your girlfriend. You have an appointment with the cat o'nine in Hell."

"I don't think so." He smiled, seeming much too pleased with himself.

How predictable. Ysabel sighed as his lady-friend tossed something at her and chanted.

Pivoting on one foot, she faced the wanna-be sorcer-ess. "You really should try finding a real spell book instead of relying on Google." Ysabel, while weaker on the mortal plane, had honed her powers through the centuries. She spoke only one word, "Congelado," and aimed her magic at the human. An expression of surprise on her face, the mortal froze.

Whipping back to face Pedro, Ysabel was just in time for his fist to hit her face.

Head snapping sideways, she didn't have time to recover before he hit her again, in the stomach doubling her over, gasping. Stupid mortal world. Everything hurt more out here, that and her magic just wasn't as strong as down in the Pit. Even worse, against the souls she was sent to recover, it was almost nonexistent because part of the curse made her revert to the same strength she held at death when faced with one of the souls she damned. Lucifer and his bloody clauses.

Where the fuck is Remy? She'd actually welcome his smirk and innuendos right about now.

Wrapping his hand around her braid, Pedro yanked her upright and she managed to whisper only the first consonant for a spell before he knocked her out with a head-butt.

4

It took Remy a little longer than five minutes to make his way from the roof to the balcony. The damned dog on the ninth floor with its sharp teeth needed avoiding. And the couple on the seventh, engaged in a sexual orgy involving Nutella, restraints, and a strap-on stole his attention for a moment. But he'd not come on a pleasurable, peeping Tom mission. He needed to reach his witchy partner and help her send the first of their targets back to Hell.

Once they accomplished their mission though, Remy would seriously be looking into getting home via another method. His still sore balls couldn't handle another ride on that torturous broom of hers. Although, he'd quite enjoyed the snuggling – ahem, groping – part.

Swinging onto the balcony of the condo he searched for, he cursed as he saw his witch out for the count at the hands of their target. He didn't waste any time busting through the sliding glass door. Not exactly his most noble entrance but at least it distracted the damned soul with the knife poised over his mouthy cougar.

"I don't think so." If anybody got to kill the shrew with the wicked tongue, it would be him. "Shall we dance?" he inquired with an arched brow. Hands held out to his side, he eased the target into a false sense of security. Remy appeared unarmed. Appearances could be so deceiving.

"I am not going back to Hell!"

"Care to wager?" Remy asked with an arched brow and a taunting smile.

The idiot charged him with the kitchen knife. Remy didn't move. Waiting until the last moment, he struck, one hand clamping like a vise around the wrist holding the weapon, the other jabbing forth to crush the prick's windpipe.

Gasping like a fish on land, the damned one sank to his knees. Remy shook his head. "Is that all you have? Really? Couldn't you have at least *tried* to make it sporting?"

Sighing, Remy kicked the target over to writhe in pain on the carpet while he went to fetch the witch. He muttered a heartfelt "Fuck," as he noticed the blossoming bruise on her cheek. Sure, it would heal, probably by morning if she used some magic, but still, what did it say about him that she'd gotten hurt on his watch?

Then again, her unconscious state meant he got to grope her, under the guise of patting her down for the tag needed to send the woman beater, Pedro, back to Hell. Not finding it in her pants pocket, or between her legs, he stuck his hand down her top and his fingers brushed the silkiest skin before touching the metal icon Lucifer gave her to complete the task.

Sliding it out, and wishing he'd thought to search with his mouth instead, he clutched it in one hand before scooping her into his arms. Carrying her, and enjoying the silent respite, he brought her to Pedro who crawled away making choking sounds.

Remy knelt and placed her limp hand around the token. Guiding her like a puppet, he slapped the icon onto the escaped soul. With a wheezing scream, Pedro sank in on himself, his essence suddenly sucked into a small black hole. Back to the Pit, where he belonged.

"Mission accomplished. Time to get you home, little cougar." Standing, he kept her cradled in his arms, and called himself all kinds of idiot for sadistically missing her acerbic tongue. Call him a masochist, but he liked the fact she didn't just give in to his charm, that she fought her obvious attraction to him.

Most denizens in Hell gave in to their base urges with little encouragement. That she refused intrigued him. And, unfortunately for her, made him determined to try even harder to get between her thighs.

But only once she begged for it.

Making his way back to the pool and the spot where they'd stashed her broom, he looked at her serene expression. She couldn't very well fly back unconscious.

A more gentle demon – a mentally unbalanced one in other words – would have balked at dumping her in to the cold water of the pool.

He, however, never claimed to be nice. Down she went. Crossing his arms, he waited. Up she came sputtering.

"You rotten jerk! What did you do that for?"

"Hey, if you're going to sleep on the job, there will be consequences," he admonished shaking a finger.

Her jaw worked, however nothing but a shocked stutter came out. "You, you –"

"Hot piece of demon ass?"

"No."

"Brave soldier of Hell?"

"No!"

"Number one panty dropper in the Pit?"

"Would you stop that," she screeched. "This is not funny. You dumped me in a pool. I could have drowned."

"Nah, I was keeping an eye to make sure you bobbed up. I was pretty confident those big melons of yours would keep you afloat."

She slogged up the pool steps, glaring at him, her teeth bared in a fierce scowl. "I am going to kill you."

"For what? Waking you up? You know," he eyed her up and down, noting how the fabric clung to the breasts he already knew from touch were round and perfect. "Wet is a good look for you," he said, his deadpan expression belied by the mirth that surely shone in his eyes.

Flipping her hair back, arching her back and placing a hand on a cocked hip, she looked utterly delicious. And up to something. "Looks good, but tastes even better," she smirked.

Ooh, point for the witch who made his mouth water at her naughty repartee. "Is that an invitation?"

"You're not my type."

"And what is your type? No wait. Let me guess. Hard, plastic coated and jammed full of big D batteries."

She scowled at him.

Touché. He'd hit a sore spot. Pity she kept shooting him down. He knew how to make that spot feel so much better. "Here's your ride." Pulling her broom out from its hiding spot, he handed it to her.

Straddling it, she barked, "What are you waiting for? Get on."

"No thanks. I'd rather not end up splattered on some city street. I'd say we're done for the night, unless you need me for some nefarious fun?"

"In your dreams, demon."

"Oh goody. I have a great imagination. I can't wait to see what you're going to do to me." He laughed when she growled. "Ooh, now that's a sexy sound. Love it. Think of me tonight when you're riding your plastic friend. I know I'll be picturing you when I'm getting off."

"I hate you."

"Do you always repeat yourself? Maybe your age is catching up to you. Good thing you've got me helping you out or you might forget your quest. So, same time tomorrow?"

"Same time for what?"

"Meeting up with you, of course, to hunt some more souls. I'll see you at your place around nine-ish."

"Not if I can help it," she muttered before taking off on her broom, a trail of liquid dripping under her.

What a woman. He couldn't remember the last time he'd found himself so intrigued. But he wouldn't get to enjoy the witch for long if she had her way. Remy revised his plan to find some mortal pussy before heading back to hell. For some reason, it suddenly became more important to make sure he stayed partnered with the witch.

You are not getting rid of me that easy.

Perhaps he'd inherited his mother's crazy gene after all. She would be so proud.

LUCIFER EYED REMY AS HE LOUNGED IN THE CHAIR ACROSS from his desk, appearing like the poster boy for insouciance, and yet, he could see the telltale anxiety in the way his one foot kept tapping. It only took Ysabel one day to screw with one of his finest trackers. Lucifer fought an urge to shake his head. "Let me get this straight. After pissing Ysabel off, to the point she's going to come storming in here any minute demanding I fire you, you still want to work with her? Are you insane?"

"I hope so," Remy grinned.

A smile cracked Lucifer's face. "Congratulations. Your mother will be ecstatic. Consider it done. I like a male who doesn't back down in the face of a shrew."

"Bah, she's not a shrew. Just a little feisty. Besides, I think I might enjoy taming a cougar with claws."

"Taming? Ysabel?" Lucifer almost choked.

"Hmm, maybe you're right. Keeping her wild will be more fun. Think I can get her to redirect that energy of hers so she stalks me and shreds the clothes from me? No, wait. She's not a shapeshifter, which means she'd need a knife. On second thought, I'll make sure I'm naked when she does decide to come after me. It's probably safer."

"Are you sure you're okay, soldier?"

"Never better, sir. Now if you'll excuse me, I shall exit via the back because if I'm not mistaken, that squelching noise signals the arrival of my hot tempered witch. Remember, I was never here."

"Never here," Lucifer muttered. Remy slipped out the secret entrance and Lucifer sighed. "What have I done?" With little time to ponder that question, he just had time to settle himself more comfortably in his seat before a sopping wet, and extremely pissed, Ysabel came stomping into his office.

"I demand you fire him."

"What? No hello?"

"Fuck you. You knew I was coming. I want him gone."

How interesting. It seemed he'd finally found someone to rile his normally collected assistant's feathers. "No can do. You need a partner."

"Then find me someone else."

"Sorry, but he's all I've got for the moment."

"But I hate him!" she yelled. Her outburst surprised them both, and it took a few blinks before the red in her cheeks died down. "Surely, there's someone else? Anyone. What about that serious demon, what's his name again, Xaphan? Couldn't I take him instead?"

"I've got plans for him." Plans Xaphan would absolutely hate. Lucifer couldn't wait.

"I am so not voting for you when the contest for boss of the year comes around," she threatened, pivoting and stomp-squishing her way back out.

"What? And here I had a speech prepared thanking myself for my greatness and the fact I did everything on my own."

Ysabel flicked him a middle finger salute before she slammed his door shut.

He smiled. *Saucy witch. If I didn't know better, I'd think she was one of my own children.*

Then again, given how she drove him nuts, he was kind of glad she wasn't. He had enough to handle with Muriel and his constantly disappearing son, Christopher. The latter he'd given up on. The former he secretly adored, especially since she'd given him a granddaughter who thought he could do no good. Which reminded him, he needed to find the pet dragon he'd bought the little tyke. It escaped its caretaker and the last thing the entire world needed was for the atomic bomb, also known as his darling granddaughter, to go off because he lost her favorite pet. Then again, the end of the world would definitely liven things up around Hell. *But cut into my golf game. Fuck.* He needed to find that dragon.

5

YSABEL TRIED to prepare herself the following afternoon when the time of her death came around. She filled the tub with cold water and climbed in naked. The shocking temperature instantly had her teeth chattering. *I can do this. Think of it as a hot day on the Hade's Beach.*

It didn't work. The flames arrived right on time, licking up her legs, her body, until they reached her head. But by then, she was already screaming, the tub full of steam. People could boast of bravery and handling pain all they wanted. No one could withstand this kind of agony, even if it petered out when its two minutes were up. She lay for a moment afterward in the tub, its water evaporated from the inferno that raged a minute before. While not a mark remained of her ordeal, her mind and body still reacted as if she suffered. The pain lingered like a bad hangover and her psyche shrieked, rejecting all attempts at calm. It sucked. *And this blast from my past is going to keep happening every day until I catch the other four souls.* It made her want to cry, a weak indulgence she'd not allowed herself since death.

She still remembered with disgust her first day in Hell. Weak, sobbing and afraid. Despite the contract she'd signed with Lucifer and her second chance at life, albeit in the Pit, she'd shivered, miserable and fearful. The memory of the flames mocked her every time she closed her eyes.

Nefertiti, Lucifer's sorceress, took one look at her and brought her home. Under her care, Ysabel learned to protect herself, her magic becoming strong enough to protect her from most of the predators in Hell. Confidence restored, she got her revenge on those who condemned her to burn, dragging five souls, the number she'd bargained for, straight to Hell, laughing as they screamed.

The hardest of the captures though, much as it shamed her, was Francisco's.

She still recalled that day, all those years ago, when she rode a broom from the portal in the woods to the village she'd grown up in. The village that denounced her.

How benign it seemed. How quaint with its thatched cottages, and dirt paths lined with gardens. But she didn't linger, even if her fingers itched to douse it in flames. She swooped with purpose to the big house on the hill, its windows dark as its occupants slept, the hour late. Landing on the sill of the window to her ex-lover's room, she slipped inside and padded on bare feet to the large bed, a bed they'd never trysted in. No, all she merited were grassy fields, and her straw filled pallet. Sometimes she didn't even get such softness, as he often liked to take her braced against a tree, her skirts flipped up so he could quickly take his pleasure. And while those brief moments left her unsatisfied, she allowed them for love.

How foolish of her to not recognize the signs of his selfishness.

Amidst the mound of pillows and bedding, he snored softly. In repose, his features were smooth, his tousled hair dark and silky to the touch. A pang of longing struck her. Why did things have to turn out this way? What evil had she truly done other than to love this man?

She must have made a sound, or the chill of her presence alerted him, because his eyes flicked open. For a long moment, he stared at her unblinking, then confusion set in and his brow creased.

"Ysabel?"

"Funny how you remember me now, yet couldn't when you watched me burn," she replied with a bitterness she couldn't stem.

"I had nothing to do with it. It was my mother."

The excuse angered her. "And you did nothing to stop it! How could you? I thought you loved me?"

Shifting his body, he sat up. "Love you? A peasant with no dowry? No land or title?" A sneer tilted his features into someone ugly. Why had she not noticed the cruelty in his face before? Not recognized his lies? "Is it my fault you were stupid enough to believe I would tie myself to someone like you?"

A part of her must have known he didn't care, known he led her on falsely, yet to hear him so baldly state it… To have him throw her stupidity in her face. She struggled against the tears at her naivety, and let the anger at his duplicity take over. "You miserable excuse for a man. I can't believe I ever let you touch me with those lying lips."

"You did. And you loved it. It's a shame mother found out about us. While inexperienced, you were quite an eager learner. At least she saved me the trouble of ridding myself of you later."

Any last doubt at her choice evaporated. "Stupid, stupid man. Did your mother never teach you not to mess with a witch?"

He dared to mock. "You're dead. You can do nothing to me now. Go ahead. Moan to your heart's content or shake your chains. You're dead and buried in an unmarked grave. Although, you can find it by looking for the dead grass that I've killed pissing on it. Go back to Hell, evil spirit, where you belong."

His attempt to rile her up didn't make her explode with anger. She went past that straight into glee. She laughed. Not a nice laugh or a hysterical one. A low chuckle, a fearless one, tinted with a touch of madness, slipped past her lips. "Oh, I'll return to Hell, Francisco, but I'm not going alone."

The knife she brought, an ebony etched blade her new friend gifted her, flashed down before he could even grasp her intent. And she thrust again and again until he gurgled his last. Seeing his soul rise from his body, still wearing a look of surprise, she blew him a kiss.

Finally losing his arrogant expression, he called her foul names and reached for her. His ghostly fingers grasped at nothing as Hell's reaper came for him. Panicked, he tried to evade his fate. But no one escaped Death on a mission, especially not a soul as dark as Francisco's. Oh how he screamed as he left the mortal plane.

But even hearing his screams, sometimes even causing them, never erased the pain of his betrayal. Never restored her ability to trust. But it sure did make her smile.

Memories of her past were interrupted as someone knocked at her repaired, and now steel reinforced, door.

"Go away," she muttered, lifting herself from the tub with limbs that reflected every one of her five hundred years. Funny how getting burned alive could make her feel so old.

She grabbed a robe and wrapped it around her frame before tottering into her bedroom. The pounding came again, along with a muffled shout. She ignored it in favor of scrounging through her underwear drawer. Yanking on her black briefs and matching athletic bra, she'd just turned to her closet when the loud bang occurred. It didn't surprise her to see Remy in her bedroom doorway a moment later.

Sighing, she turned her back to him and kept fingering the clothes in her closet.

"Hello, little witch."

"You're early."

"I couldn't wait to see you."

Now why did his casually tossed words have to make her heart flutter? So unfair, especially since she knew he didn't mean them. "Just so you know, I'm sending you the bill for the repair of the door again."

"Yeah, I meant to ask you why you did that."

She flashed him an incredulous look. "Seriously? You broke it down. Twice now."

"I wouldn't have to keep forcing my way in if you'd answer the damned thing."

"Did it ever occur to you that I was occupied?"

Sniffing the air, he grimaced. "Busy doing what?

Barbecuing? Smells like charred flesh and burnt hair in here? Have you been indulging in some kind of weird witch ritual?"

So, Lucifer hadn't told him of her curse. Good. Flirty Remy she could handle. Joking Remy too. A Remy who felt sorry for her? That would just piss her off. More than usual, at any rate.

"What you smell is what happens when people fuck with me." What do you know? She managed to tell the truth, if not in the manner he expected. Lucifer was probably grinding his teeth in his office.

"You set them on fire? I'd be willing to burn for a taste of what's between your thighs."

She ground her teeth. "I hate you."

"Is that any way to speak to your future lover?"

Suddenly tired of sparring, the ordeal still fresh in her mind, her shoulders slumped. As if sensing her mood, he changed the subject to something, gasp, nonsexual.

"So my little cougar, which target are we after today?"

That she had an answer to. "Emmanuelle. A little demon who cleans her cell told me," after she tortured the information out of him, "she has a rather keen interest in her heirs. Especially the oldest daughters, who, over the years, inherited the bakery Emmanuelle took over after she killed her husband." The bitch had screamed to all who would listen that it was Ysabel's fault the bread wouldn't rise, instead of blaming the true reason – improperly stored yeast.

Once in Hell and planning her revenge, Ysabel also became privy to the knowledge that Francisco was fucking the baking whore on the side. She'd quite enjoyed shoving Emmanuelle into the oven and slamming the door shut when she'd gone to collect the bitch's soul.

"So we're off to Spain. Excellent. I've been meaning to practice my Spanish." The leer on his lips and shine in his eyes let her know he didn't mean the language.

"We're not leaving yet. It's not quite nine p.m. over there. I figure we'll most likely catch Emmanuelle in the morning when her heirs begin their baking day. So we've got about six hours to wait."

"I've got an idea to kill a few hours."

"I doubt what you have in mind will take more than a few minutes."

"Only because you excite me so much, but that wasn't what I was suggesting. Something about the method your little friends escaped the prison is bugging me. I thought maybe you'd like to come along and help me check it out."

Okay, that totally surprised her. One, that he'd looked into it, and two, that he even gave a shit. It roused her suspicion. "Why do you care?"

The grin he flashed her, pure and masculine, shot right to her sex and tickled. "I hate a mystery. Besides, if there's a security breach, I want to know. Escaped slaves mean more work, which means less play time for me."

"And we can't have that now, can we?" She pulled out a pantsuit, appropriate for investigating a prison. Well, not really, but she wasn't about to wear something sexy for the jerk when he'd not deigned to notice she stood there in only her underwear while they spoke.

Or did he?

A fingertip trailed down her spine and she whirled only to see him still leaning against her doorjamb, his lips quirked in a half smile, his eyes half lidded. "Yes?"

"Did you just touch me?"

He spread his hands in a gesture of 'who, me?' "How, when I'm standing over here?"

"I need to get dressed."

"I'd rather you didn't."

"Says the man who managed to speak several coherent sentences without trying to get my panties off."

"Would you have taken them off if I asked?"

"No."

"Then why ask when I could fantasize? The entire time we were talking, with your hot cougar body borderline naked, I was thinking of how I'd peel that prim and proper underwear from you with my teeth. If we'd have kept talking, who knows how far we would have gotten. Although, from the little bit I imagined, I have to say, you are a very, very naughty witch." Oh now there was a masculine grin to make even her melt.

She spun before he could see her answering blush. Harder to hide were the nipples poking through her cups, and the moisture wetting the crotch of her panties. *Please don't' tell me he's one of those demons with a wicked sense of smell.*

"I'll be waiting in the other room."

Stunned he'd leave so easily, she whirled around but he was gone. Hmph. Figuring out his quick mood switches occupied her mind while she finished dressing. But she forewent the pantsuit for a short black skirt with pleats, a low cut red blouse and fishnet stockings.

Perusing her appearance in the mirror after, she smirked. Just because she didn't want him didn't mean she shouldn't torture him.

It seemed she'd finally found a pastime she enjoyed –

sparring with Remy. *But how far am I willing to take this battle of words?* For some reason, the words *all the way*, sprang to mind.

———

PACING IN YSABEL'S LIVING ROOM, REMY ONCE AGAINST castigated himself for the madness leading him to beg Lucifer to keep him paired with the witch. He only had to picture her looking delicious in her proper underclothes – which begged to be ripped off – to know why.

Fuck, did he want her. His restraint in the face of the temptation she posed surprised him. With most females, he would have attempted a kiss by now. Or a full on seduction that never, ever failed. But with his feisty witch, he didn't dare. Despite the sweet scent of her arousal, oh yes, he'd not missed it, he doubted she'd give in so easily.

So he backed off, disarmed her when she thought she had him pegged. Little did she know, the very things she accused him of were what he would have done in normal circumstances. However, there was nothing normal about his cougar.

Speaking of which, what the fuck happened before he arrived? He'd not just busted down the door because she didn't answer. He could have sworn as he travelled the corridors leading to her suite that he heard screaming. Female screaming. *Ysabel.* He'd run the rest of the way and when she wouldn't answer, he busted in, ready to commit murder, only he found her looking fetching in her under-wear, though pale, with lines of pain bracketing her mouth and eyes.

Something or someone had hurt her. And yet, she was

alone, the smells in her place belonging only to her and the weird burning scent which faded as he conversed with her.

She hid something, of that he'd wager, but what?

He'd find out sooner or later. And if it hurt her, he'd kick its ass.

First things first, though – investigating the prison where the souls she'd paid to have tortured resided.

Some would think it was unfair for one person to be able to sell their soul to the Devil in return for eternal punishment of others. And to be clear, it wasn't allowed in all requests. In order for the exchange to work, the soul asking for vengeance needed just cause. Remy didn't have access to Ysabel's file, buried in his Lord's private vault, but if she'd managed to get numerous souls condemned to the worst Hell had to offer, then they must have fucked up royally.

Knowing they must have hurt her, and bad, pissed him right off. Never mind he didn't know her when it happened. Or that she pretended to dislike him now. He now felt like he had a vested interest in making sure those who'd done her harm got punished, starting with the being who aided five of them in escaping.

Why do that? And more importantly, who? Who possessed that kind of clout and more importantly, wanted to screw with his witch?

Remy intended to find out. And then he'd fuck them up.

6

HELL BORE MANY FACES, the most common that of a sprawling metropolis with a scenic background of smoking mountains and raining ash. But Hell was more than its tenement housing, dilapidated castles and winding, dusty roads. The pit was growing constantly. Literally. It kept expanding to greater and greater size despite the wild jungles surrounding the ever widening nine circles. No matter how many cartographers tried to map the ever changing landscape, unexplored territory kept cropping up, dangerous places that few returned from.

But, if one ignored the Pit's magical ability to accommodate all the souls, demons and other beings that kept arriving and multiplying, then you could see just how normal it actually was.

In many ways, Hell resembled the mortal plane, which would have surely disappointed secular scholars. Housing and rambling streets littered the nine circles. Buildings of all shapes and sizes, including stores and theaters, cropped up wherever a spot could accommodate it. Hell had it all, built by the damned looking to make the Pit feel like home. A home for those that sinned only a little at any rate.

There was one aspect of the eternally hot plane that would have delighted those who preached of fire and brimstone; the prisons.

Hell knew how to punish. Made an art of it and reveled in it. The screams of agony and pleas for mercy echoed long before the twining trail leading to the establishment, known simply as Hell's Prison, ended. Fear not though – while most souls were destined to live in the Pit, only the really spectacular ones earned punishment and imprisonment.

Rapists, serial murderers, corporate leaders, lawyers – all suffered the eternal agonies for the misdeeds they'd performed in life. Lucifer, with so many souls to shepherd, saved his best for the worst.

The rusted, metal gates flanked by guard towers loomed into view and the agonized shrieks increased in pitch. Remy glanced at his witch to see her reaction, but she didn't cringe or shy away. She marched alongside him, cool and imperious, unafraid and unashamed of what went on beyond the prison doors. Obviously, she'd visited this vile place before, but he wondered for what purpose.

The warden, a corpulent demon covered in black pustules met with them, his yellow, slitted eyes lingering overly long on Ysabel's curvy frame. Remy allowed the visual admiration, but if he dared touch... A possessive streak for the witch surprised him. Jealousy was not something he'd encountered often, and never for a female. Job promotion or cool digs, yes, but a woman?

It was probably because she refused him. He saw her

as a challenge and until he got into her pants, he didn't want anyone else getting a taste of his prize. Oh yeah, that was a big fat lie. His boss was probably so proud.

"Remy, Lucifer's own guard. What brings you to our fine establishment?" said the warden, recognizing him.

Surprised, Remy looked harder at the demon, then smiled. "Crax, you old bugger. So this is where you ended up?" He almost didn't recognize Crax, the emaciated youth he once knew now enormous in size.

"After the academy," where all demons, full, half or quarter went when still in their teens, "my Lord assigned me to the prison, but it's only recently I earned my promotion."

"Congrats on running the place. Nice gig," Remy congratulated. Personally, more than a few hours in this place and he'd probably go mad and end up drooling in a corner. It took a tough stomach and mind to work in a place like this.

His old school chum puffed up his chest. "Thank you. But since you didn't know I was here, something else obviously brought you."

"I'm here on behalf of our Lord. I am investigating the escape of five of your prisoners." And there went Crax's jovial smile, which, for the uninitiated was more frightening than the scowl he currently sported.

"Those bloody fuckers. We got one of them back last night. He's getting reacquainted with the rack as we speak."

"Did you question him on how he escaped?" Ysabel asked before Remy could.

Crax's yellow gaze took her in before he answered. "I asked. He won't answer. Some kind of spell is stopping him. I've called in the Lord's witch to take a look since my resident magikers can tell me nothing."

"Might we have a turn? My lady friend and I have an interest in the case and have our Lord's permission to investigate."

"Be my guest."

Crax led them through a warren of hallways, some of the archways branching off, showing scenes of fire and torture, others whipping, some skinning, and one strange one involving tickling.

The warden saw Remy ogling and chuckled. "That there psycho thinks that laughter is a sin. Killed the neighbor's kids because they kept giggling in their yards. So, we spend all day making him laugh. You should hear the chap sobbing in his cell at night as he beats his head on the wall."

Yeah, like he said, Lucifer excelled at what he did.

Entering a part of the building that seemed awfully quiet compared to the rest of their journey, Remy frowned. "Do you have silence dampening spells on this section?"

Crax shook his head. "I told you that Pedro fellow wasn't talking. And I mean at all. Not a scream or peep no matter what we do. It's freaking the boys out."

It freaked him out, never mind the others, and flicking a quick glance at Ysabel, he saw the troubled line on her forehead.

They entered a chamber, well lit with fluorescent lights which made the scene shine in all its gory details. Suffice it to say, it was nasty, even by his standards, and bloody, hence the drains in the floor.

Ysabel stepped daintily over the red rivulets inching

their way down into Hell's plumbing until she stood in front of a large rack. Splayed, spread eagle and raw, like meat skinned for a spit, was their friend from the night before, Pedro, and he didn't look like a happy resident of the Pit which suited Remy just fine. Scumbags deserved punishment.

Despite the lack of noise, only a blind idiot wouldn't notice that Pedro suffered. His eyes bulged. His mouth hung open in a silent scream, but nothing, not even the hiss of air could be heard. It wasn't right. Even mutes made noise.

Remy watched as his witch eyed the man up and down, then sketched some symbols in the air. He caught a hint of magic, the ozone scent and electrifying tingle giving her attempts away. The scene didn't change and it remained quiet enough to keep even a baby demon sleeping.

After a few moments, she turned, appearing pensive. "Whatever has him bound is strong. And subtle. I can't even see the threads to the spell preventing him from speaking."

"Which means he definitely had some kind of outside aid in escaping."

"Impossible," sputtered Crax. "We monitor visitors closely. Frisk them more thoroughly than their lovers."

"You can't see magic though," she advised dryly.

Crax scowled at her observation.

"We'll need copies of the visitor logs," Remy ordered. "And I want to see their cells. Maybe their mysterious benefactor left a clue."

"Of course. Follow me."

Ysabel strode after Crax, and Remy dropped back,

more to admire her ass than anything else. Round, with enough cushion for the pushing, he couldn't wait to –

"It looks even better bent over," she tossed over her shoulder. "Not that you'll ever see that. I save that for my special friends." She laughed, a husky sound that went straight to his cock and stroked him. Then the minx added a little extra wiggle to her walk. Like he said before, his Lord knew how to torture, even his favored soldiers.

They visited five solitary cells – stone walls, no window, seamless rock for the floor, thick metal bars for a door – bare of everything, even a blanket.

"There's nothing here," Remy growled as he paced the last one. Not even a misplaced scent.

"No magic," she mused running her fingers over the stone blocks. "No carved messages. Nothing. How did they escape again?"

Crax shrugged. "We've yet to figure that one out. One moment, they was all in their cells crying for the abyss, the next time we checked, they was gone. The doors still locked, not a single alarm tripped."

"What about the video footage?"

A glob of spittle hit the floor and sizzled before Crax answered. "Fucking wiped. The whole lot of them. And before you ask, no, we have no idea how the fuck it happened. Bloody imps most likely, though. The pesky buggers get into everything."

"So let me get this straight," Ysabel asked. "You lost five prisoners, have no idea how or when, have no video footage due to some malfunction, and you can't even make one chained up soul talk?"

"When you put it that way, it sounds bad."

Ysabel stepped up to the warden and although she

remained shorter than him by almost a foot, she seemed to grow somehow in presence. "What's bad is if you let any more prisoners escape, the Devil won't have to fire you because I'll come down here myself, carve your body parts off one at a time and feed them to the hounds. Incompetence is unacceptable and I will not tolerate it."

"Yes, ma'am."

Remy laughed as Crax reeled back from her, a dazed look on his face. He was still chuckling as they exited the rusted gates.

"What is so damned funny?" she asked through gritted teeth.

"You. I mean, you couldn't even hold your own against Pedro last night and yet you're threatening the warden of Hell's Prison. That takes balls."

He received no warning, just a flick of her hand and he went flying, his impromptu airborne status halted by a crag of rock. And not a smooth one. Ouch.

Ysabel stalked toward him, hips undulating, power weaving around her frame lifting her curls in a wild dance. Stuck like a bug, her magic binding him in place, he enjoyed the view of his witch having a tantrum. Talk about hot.

"First off, demon, let's get one thing straight. I. Am. Not. Weak. What you saw last night was another fucking subclause of Lucifer's that makes me of the same strength physically and magically as when I died, but only when on the mortal plane in the presence of the souls I damned. Any other time, I am not to be messed with."

"If you're so bad ass, how come I never heard of you?"

"I prefer to stay out of the spotlight, unlike some

sorceress's I know," she said with a smile as she came to stop in front of him. "But I do have a nickname."

"Hot on a stick?"

"No."

"Spanks with magic?"

"Most definitely not."

"I know, you must be the famous BJ Swallows."

"I am going to hurt you."

"I was right?"

"No. And your made up names are just pissing me off."

"Made up? I'll have you know those monikers are just a few of the more famous witch ones I know. Of course, I don't know if their magical abilities extend beyond the pole they dance on, but still, they're very well known in my circles."

"Why am I not surprised?"

"Are you going to tell what your name is then? 'Cause I'm gonna wager it isn't Magical Pie."

He really needed to learn how to keep certain thoughts to himself, an easy thing to promise with the iron grip she had on his balls. Not exactly how he pictured their first time touching.

She twisted. He winced. "Let this be a reminder not to fuck with me. And just so you know, while my nickname is the Blood Witch, my true title is Satan's Assistant."

She was the one who had all the damned souls trembling? Hot damn. "I *have* heard of you."

"Good, then you know what I can do. And might I add it hurts." She leaned up on tiptoe as she said it, her lips so close to his.

But Ysabel wasn't the only one with surprises. And truly, she'd pushed the boundaries of temptation too far.

He snapped her magic binding and wrapped his arms around her, bringing her flush against his chest. "Did I mention, apart from ability with fire, I can unravel several forms of magic?" Then he kissed her, and by all the coals in the furnace of Hell, he'd never burned hotter.

———

HOW DID I GO FROM PUTTING HIM IN HIS PLACE TO HAVING HIS tongue in my mouth?

An interesting question for sure, but not as intriguing as the fire he ignited. While Ysabel on a few occasions – usually drunk –let other men kiss her –before she decked them with magic –nothing compared to Remy's embrace. Not even Francisco's kiss.

How he could suck her lower lip and make her feel it between her legs was a mystery – one she enjoyed. How he could curl his tongue around hers and wring a pleasurable shudder from her body made no sense. His hands cupped her bottom, squeezing her cheeks, pressing her against his firm body. A body excited to feel hers, judging by the hard bulge nudging her belly.

The moment was one of utter madness – and arousal. She wanted to rip the shirt from him and drag her nails down his torso. She wanted him to hoist her so she could wrap her legs around his waist and…

She tore her mouth from his and shoved at his chest. "What have you done to me?"

Eyes glittering with desire, he regarded her. "I kissed you."

"Obviously. But how did you make me enjoy it? Kisses aren't supposed to make me feel like, like –"

"You're a beautiful, desirable woman in need of man's touch? Aching to feel his –"

"Don't you dare say it! I don't want you. I don't even like you. So again, what kind of magic did you use? Or is it a drug?"

He smirked. "It's called expert technique, little cougar. For an experienced woman of your years, I would have thought you'd know that."

She refused to blush or avert her gaze. "I've been with men before." Actually, a single man, who while capable of giving her pleasure, ended up betraying her. Apart from her education with Francisco, her only comparison came from drunken fumblings that never went further than sloppy kisses, which she followed by a rinse with 99% proof liquor to wash out any residue. "This was nothing like that."

"Thank you. Shall we continue?"

"No. And don't you do what you did to me again."

"It's called a French kiss."

"Whatever. Try it again and I'll –" *Bend over and beg you to take me. Scream as you tongue my pussy. Fuck you until –* "Argh! I hate you."

Stomping away wasn't one of her shining moments, especially since she felt his gaze boring into her backside, and damn it all if it didn't make her add an extra wiggle.

I need to get him away from me before I do something stupid. Yeah, like orgasm with something not made of plastic for the first time in five hundred years.

———

LUCIFER LINED UP HIS SHOT AND GAVE A FEW PRACTICE

swings with his number nine thigh bone. The shrunken skull waited for him to putt. He pulled back and –

"I demand you castrate him!"

– his shot went wild, careening off the pillars and missing his interior putting green entirely. Sighing, he turned and faced Ysabel, who, as usual, appeared annoyed.

"What has he done this time?" he asked as she flopped into a chair.

"He kissed me."

He'd always known Remy was braver than most. "The horror. The shame. And?"

"What do you mean, *and*? I didn't want him to."

"So tell him no."

"I did. Kind of." He stared at her. She sighed. "Fine, I kissed him back. But I didn't want to. He made me do it."

Lucifer blinked. Stuck a finger in his ear and wiggled it. Surely he misunderstood. "He made you do it? I'm sorry, did I suddenly enter an alternate universe? Since when does anyone make you do anything? I've been trying to get you to show up on time for five hundred years and you still insist on making your own hours."

A smirk graced her face. "I do it to keep you on your toes. But, back to the kissing demon. I want to know how to stop him from using his magic or potion or whatever it was he used to make me like it."

Now this was interesting. "You're mad because you enjoyed it?"

"Loved it, actually," Remy announced, striding in unannounced. It seemed his witch's bad habits were rubbing off.

"Does no one knock anymore?" But they weren't paying Lucifer any attention as they faced off.

"I did not like it."

"Liar. The tongue in my mouth said otherwise."

"I was pushing yours out."

"Then what were the moans of pleasure?"

"I did not moan."

"Mmm. Mmm." Remy closed his eyes and adopted a blissful expression with puckered lips.

It occurred to Lucifer as Ysabel raised her fingers that he might want to take cover.

"I am going to turn you into an imp," she threatened.

"Touch me in a non-erotic way and I am telling you right now, I will consider it foreplay, and not only will I kiss you again, I will strip every piece of clothing from you, lick you from head to toe, and make you scream my name, not once, not twice, but three times as you come."

"You wouldn't dare," she huffed, her eyes flashing with ire – and more intriguing to Lucifer, interest.

Before they could cause any damage, to his office at any rate, Lucifer snapped his fingers and froze them. He didn't really care what they did to each other, but he'd spent several months in the wild capturing the beast he'd turned into a desk.

"Children, children," he said tucking his hands behind his back and adopting his father figure mode. It usually made his daughter, Muriel, laugh. "Must I remind you that I tasked you with a mission. One that I might add, Ysabel, you should be most eager to complete. What I do not need, is for you to FUCK IT UP!" He let his voice increase in treble until it boomed. "I've been more than tolerant, but enough is enough. You will cease bringing me your petty squabbles. You will do the job I assigned. And if you don't want his tongue in your mouth, Ysabel, then bite it off. Although, really, if you enjoyed it so much, I don't see what the problem is. Maybe he can help you remove the stick up your ass if you let him kiss the other end. Now, if we're done here, and since I'm boss, and I say we are, leave and don't come back until you're done, because if you do, I'm duct taping the pair of you together and throwing you in a dark room until you learn to get along. Or fuck. I don't really care which, but I prefer the latter so I can watch."

A snap of his fingers, and the glaring pair, stalked off, silent for the moment, but he'd wager it would only last until they hit the hall.

And right on cue...

"I've never seen a stick up a butt before. Wanna bend over and show me?" Whack. "Ow, that was totally uncalled for."

Lucifer sighed as he slumped in his chair instead of practicing his shot. At the rate things were going, his machinations would never bear fruit and even worse, his brother would kick his ass at their centennial Golf Across the Planes tournament. Like Hell.

7

Leaning against a counter, Remy watched as Ysabel paced the bakery. She'd not said much since they left Lucifer's office, not even to protest his renting of a motorcycle versus riding her ball torturer. It was totally ruining his fun. Although, he'd quite enjoyed the trip, taking the corners extra fast and sharp just so she'd hold on tighter. He'd met pythons with weaker grips.

But, he'd not counted on helmets – stupid mortal laws – and the engine noise rendering conversation impossible. A shame, because he really enjoyed verbally sparring with her. With this in mind, he kept talking, knowing she'd eventually snap out of her uncommunicative mode and give it to him. *Just like I'd love to give it to her, naked.*

"So when do you figure she'll show up?" He watched her pacing figure as he queried, her outfit of before changed from a skirt to hip hugging jeans, a t-shirt that read, "Touch me and DIE!" and a jean jacket that went out of style in the eighties.

"Hmm, probably around three or four a.m. so she can

arrive before her great times a million granddaughter shows up, which is exactly what I told you five minutes ago."

"What can I say? I love the sound of your voice." He grinned when she scowled. "But seriously though –"

"Is that even possible with you?"

"Give me a chance and I'll show you."

The snort she emitted probably didn't have a heading in the handbook of 'How To Act Like A Lady', but he thought it cute anyway. Just all part of her witchy charm. "What do you say when this is all over, we go out on a date. Dinner, drinks, maybe some dancing."

"Is that another euphemism for sex?"

"No. But, if you'd like to throw that into the ring, I'm going on the record as saying I'm fine with it." He flashed a wide smile and caught her biting her lip to prevent herself from grinning back. *Whether she'll admit it or not, I'm growing on her.*

"What is it with you? Why are you so determined to get between my legs? Is it because I didn't drop my panties and beg you to take me? Is it the challenge?"

"Nah. You're not the first to play hard to get." He wiggled his brows when she choked. "Although, you have lasted longer than most. Honestly, I think you're kind of cool for a witch." Cool, intriguing, sexy, and more. She consumed all his thoughts, awake and asleep. His new mission in life involved learning everything about her – likes, dislikes. Did she sleep naked? Did she cry or cheer at the end of Old Yeller? Was she a snuggler? A folder or crinkler?

This kind of thirst for a woman, that involved things other than sex, shocked him. It made him wonder why her? Why now? The answer eluded him, but he knew one thing for sure. *I want this witch.* And he wanted her to want him, too.

"I'm cool? Gee, be still my racing heart. With that kind of compliment, how could I not want to spread my thighs?" She rolled her eyes. "We have nothing in common and I am not into casual sex."

"Have you tried it? Because I can totally recommend it." Although, he had a sneaking suspicion, once, twice, even a million times with her would never quench his lust.

"I'll bet you can. No thank you. The single life suits me fine."

"Says the girl who has double D batteries smuggled in by the case." He snickered when her jaw hit the floor. "Before you ask, I have my sources. Now just what could those be for? Flashlight? Seems unlikely, given you can snap your fingers and create light. Boom box? No, those went out in the eighties. What does that leave?"

Hopping up onto a steel countertop, Ysabel smiled at him. "Fine. I admit it. It's for Big D. Nine inches, thick, and with a vibrating setting guaranteed to make me cream. When I'm in a hurry and in the mood, I don't even use lube with him. I just pop him into my mouth like this." Inserting her middle finger, she sucked it, slow and sensuous. Remy wanted to drop to his knees and drool.

"I get it nice and wet before rubbing it across here." She cupped herself through her jeans and he desperately wanted his mouth to take the place of her hand. "I try to shove it in, but it's so big, and I'm so tight. I have to work it, twisting and pushing." She gyrated her hips. "Deeper and deeper." She licked her lips. "It feels so good."

Did the surprises with her never end? "Yes. Yes. Don't stop now." He could so easily picture what she orated, but he substituted his cock for the vibrator. Oh to feel her lips on him. Or her tight sheath as he pushed his way in.

"I come. The end. And the best part about Big D is he never talks back."

"I'd let you gag me if that would help. Fuck, tie me down and just let me watch."

She blew him a kiss. "You wish. Now if you're done probing me about my sex life, can we get back to the job?"

Oh, he'd love to probe her, as *part* of her sex life. But duty called. "The job is here."

"What?"

Having heard with senses other than his ears the arrival of something not completely mortal, Remy put a finger on his lips and motioned her to silence. Standing on opposite sides of the swinging door leading to the storefront area, they waited.

The soul didn't open the portal to enter, but misted, appearing suddenly in the kitchen area. Despite the petite female figure, Remy pounced and...caught a handful of nothing.

Their target rematerialized several feet away, her dark eyes flashing. "I don't think so, demon."

"Oh, I do Emmanuelle." Ysabel moved toward the damned one, determination on her face.

"Oh, if it isn't the witch. Still pissy about the whole Francisco mess? Really, you should get over it. He wasn't even that good of a fuck."

How interesting. For the first time, hearing about Francisco's infidelity didn't give her a painful pang. "Nice to see you're still as classy as ever. Now are you going to do this the easy way, or are you going to make my day and run? I'd just love an excuse to hurt you."

"Puta! I am not going back to that prison. I don't deserve to be punished. I did nothing wrong."

"Nothing but sleep with everyone not married to you *and* accuse me of witchcraft."

"Again. So long ago. I've forgotten it. You should try it too. If you'll excuse me, I've got much better places to be." Emmanuelle misted.

With a curse, Ysabel grabbed a powdered sugar shaker and tossed it, scattering fine dust everywhere and coating the floating fog. Remy caught on and peered around before settling on a jar of cherry juice. He dumped it over the ball of white powder and it sank as the particles soaked up the liquid.

"Keep her busy," Ysabel commanded as she began to chant.

Keep a sticky ball of air busy, right. How the fuck was he supposed to do that? He started grabbing everything he could find and dumping it on the creeping, discorporeal spirit. Nothing he did completely stopped her implacable trek to the outside door. Nor could he grab on and hold her, his hands went right through the rainbow colored cloud and emerged gooey.

With a tiny burst of power, Ysabel finished her spell and Emmanuelle rematerialized, covered in goop.

With a smirk of triumph, his witch stepped up to the other woman, and punched her, a great left hook, right to the kisser.

"Woo, cat fight!" he yelled.

Shooting him a disgusted look, Ysabel grabbed the

reeling Emmanuelle by the hair and shoved her against the counter.

"Before I send you back to Hell, I've got some questions for you."

The damned soul clamped her lips tight.

Ysabel leaned in close and said in a low whisper, "Silence won't make things easier. You should know by now blood doesn't make me squeamish. Tell me who helped you escape."

Emmanuelle shook her head and Ysabel slammed her face off the counter. Remy winced at the sound of bone cracking.

"Let's try this again. Who helped you escape?"

"A purple fairy in sparkly spandex." The surprising answer saw them all blink, including Emmanuelle.

"Stop screwing around." His witch slammed her captive against the counter again and wound her fist tighter in the hair. "Who helped you escape?"

"A hippopotamus on roller blades." Emmanuelle bit her lip, her eyes wide with what Remy recognized as confusion.

"Um, Ysabel, I don't think she can answer you."

"Really?" his witch said shooting him a dark look. "Funny you should say that seeing as how she keeps flapping her gums every time I ask her."

"Yeah, but I don't think she's the one coming up with the words. Are you?"

Emmanuelle shook her head. "But even if I knew I wouldn't tell you, witch!"

Ysabel sighed, and kneed their captive in the stomach. As Emmanuelle bent over gasping, his witch shook her head. "I should have known better than to question her. No one ever tells the slag what's going on."

"Bitch," the captured soul spat. "I can't wait to hear your screams when Francisco catches up to you."

"They'll be screams of joy. Enjoy the pit. I hear Crax is most eager for your return." Ysabel slapped the straight to Hell prison icon onto her target.

Bearing a look of horror, Emmanuelle winked out of sight, but her threatening words lingered.

"I won't let anything happen to you," Remy said, puffing up his chest. "So you don't need to be worried about this Francisco fellow hurting you." For some reason, the thought of someone hurting his little cougar didn't sit well. What he liked even less was knowing this other male had, if Emmanuelle could be believed, touched his witch. *Not that it matters because once I get my hands on Ysabel, she won't even remember his name.* Yes, he was that good, or so his ego assumed. He didn't often stop to ask.

"I'm not worried about him. A puny man in life, he's an even more pathetic excuse for one in death."

"Exactly what did he do to you? That broad seemed to be implying the two of you were involved."

"None of your business. We're done here. If you don't mind, I'd like to get home."

"Going to get naked and play with Big D?"

She smirked. "Wouldn't you like to know?"

"I'd rather participate."

"In your dreams, demon."

"Oh you are, my witch, and might I add you're very naked and flexible."

"I hate you."

"And yet I bet you'll think of me when you're playing

with yourself." He knew he thought of her when he showered earlier that day. Thought of her as he stroked himself and came – twice.

"Oh, I'll be thinking of you alright," she said. "Thinking of the ways I'm going to kill you. My favorite so far is staking you down in the Pit's desert, stripping you naked –"

"Oooh, I'm liking this so far."

"Slathering you in honey."

"Yes, baby. Please tell me the next part involves a tongue."

"It does – hundreds of them as I call forth the fire lizards and present you as lunch."

He couldn't help it, despite her threats and promises of death, he laughed. And so would his mother because his witch's idea of torture resembled the courtship between his mom and step dad. *I knew she liked me!*

ARRIVING HOME AN HOUR LATER, HER CLOTHING DRY THIS time – if she ignored her panties – she tried to ditch her demon helper at the portal. Like a tick, he stuck to her side, following her home.

"I don't need you to guard me," she grumbled for the fifth time as they navigated the corridors of the palace.

"There are still three souls unaccounted for along with their mysterious benefactor."

"Only an idiot would try and accost me almost under Lucifer's nose."

"Or someone desperate."

She didn't bother replying. Since he didn't seem

inclined to budge, she let him tag along, but as they walked she couldn't help thinking about him, how he wasn't what she expected.

Despite his sexual innuendos and his one stolen kiss, he'd not pushed her or tried to take anything extra by force. And really, he wouldn't have to force her very hard, considering every time she relived the kiss, her whole body wanted to melt into a puddle. Just looking at him when he smiled at her so intimately proved a battle as she fought not to throw herself at him, tear off his clothes and do wicked, evil things.

It made no sense. Here he was, a prime example of a player, a male who used women for sex, and yet, despite this, she wanted him. Wanted him like she'd never wanted Francisco.

Maybe I've finally lost my mind.

Or, she'd finally healed enough to consider letting someone in her bed, on strict terms of course. Eyes open, she could use him for sex, that body-to-body contact she hated to admit she missed. But nothing else. No love. No relationship, just hot, sweaty –

"Home sweet home, my little cougar."

And so it was. During her musings, when she'd not paid any attention – a good way to get killed – they'd arrived at her newly repaired door.

Whirling, she forced herself to look him in the eye and say, "Thank you. I guess I'll see you tomorrow."

"Don't you mean later today?" The lazy smile he tossed her did strange things to her insides, and when his eyes darkened, an intensity filling them as he continued to stare, the tingling left her belly and travelled lower.

Did she lean toward him in invitation, or did he plan it

all along? Did it matter when the result was him sweeping her into his arms and crushing her mouth with his?

This was one time where reality outstripped fantasy. She'd not exaggerated her recollection, she realized as the inferno only he could cause swept through, leaving her aching and needing more.

At the insistent probing of his tongue, she opened her mouth, let him sweep in and plunder, unable to stop the shudders of her body or her escaping moans. His hands roamed her back, sliding up and down her shirt before moving lower to cup her buttocks. He squeezed – she gasped, a sound he caught with a chuckle.

Madness. Pure insanity. What else could explain why she necked with him in the hall? Especially with a bed not far away.

The degree of her wantonness finally shocked her back to reality and she pulled away from Remy, lips swollen and her body screaming for her to go on.

Grasping the knob to her door, she took a steadying breath before saying, "Good night."

"Don't you mean come in? And by *in*, I'm talking about that sweet spot between your legs."

And with his crude come-on line, the remainder of the seductive spell shattered. She pursed her lips. "Not necessary. I've got Big D for that, but thanks for getting me warmed up. I'd run out of lube, so the natural honey will come in handy." And with that tart rejoinder, she slammed the door in Remy's astonished face.

Safe in the haven of her home – unless he chose to batter down the door again – she waited. Listened. Not a sound came through the thick barrier. Not a knock or shudder. No splinters flying.

He left.

No, she wasn't disappointed, she thought as her shoulders slumped. Just relieved she wouldn't have to put up with him. Yeah. Right.

Feet dragging, she stripped as she headed to her bedroom, the air kissing her skin, not cooling the fever still coursing through her veins at all.

Why didn't I invite him in? He would have accepted. He would have fucked her until she went cross-eyed with pleasure. She knew that for a fact. Would have enjoyed it too. And even better, he wasn't the type to want a relationship. With him she'd get exactly what he promised. No strings sex.

And it was long overdue.

However, and herein lay the problem – could she get that close to someone without getting attached? Despite her brave taunts and boasts, and general dislike of demons, she couldn't say, not anymore at any rate, that she hated Remy. On the contrary, the more time they spent together, the more she actually liked him. Liked him, liked him. *Which is so fucking wrong.* Remy was not boyfriend material. *And I don't want a boyfriend.*

Or at least not one whose number was scrawled in every public women's washroom in Hell. *For a great fuck call...*

She sighed as she sank onto her mattress. Had loneliness finally driven her over the edge? Was she at last desperate enough for a man in her life that she imagined feelings for the worst possible candidate?

Or maybe I'm just really horny.

That was something she could fix. Grabbing Big D from her nightstand drawer, she tried to not compare his cold, plastic size to the hard bulge she recalled Remy sporting. As she slid it between her thighs, she tried not to pretend it was Remy sinking into her instead. Remy thrusting into her, fucking her, caressing her. *Loving me...*

When she cried out in climax, it was his face she saw, his name she uttered.

Lying there, her body calming, she cursed the way he'd completely captivated her mind and body. How to erase the spell? How to erase him?

The phone on her nightstand rang. Grabbing it, she snarled, "What?"

"I just wanted to ask how I was? Because you were superb," he purred.

How did he...? What did he...? Arousal came blasting back at his words, pissing her off. "Felipe was awesome."

"Who?" he growled.

"Felipe, my fuck buddy. Haven't I mentioned him before? Well, he was waiting for me inside, and mmmm." She paused for effect. "Let's just say it was screaming, creaming fun. And if you don't mind, I've got to go. It's time for round two."

The hellish buzz as he slammed the receiver down didn't please her as much as expected. And despite the fact she stayed awake for a while, the door never got busted down. Remy never arrived in a jealous rage to kick her invisible lover's ass.

The jerk.

LUCIFER BIT INTO HIS FOOT LONG DOG — A daschund/collie mix with a touch of mustard and hot sauce. Mmm, nothing like it. And to think, the mortals used ground pork and beef sausages in their version. Taking another mouthful he couldn't immediately answer when Remy plopped onto the kitchen stool beside him with a growled, "She's got a boyfriend!"

Swallowing, he tried to make sense of his soldier's words. "Who does?"

"The witch. Ysabel. I just called her to wish goodnight and she hung up on me so she could go round two with Felipe." Remy's lip and tone curled in disgust.

Nope, he couldn't help himself. Lucifer snorted, then chuckled.

"What's so funny, boss?"

"You, believing her. Ysabel hasn't been with a man since her one and only lover fucked her over." Not that Lucifer cared. Francisco's mistake earned him a five hundred year contract and a soul.

"Are you saying she made it up?"

"Felipe is the name of her cat. And last I heard, she wasn't into animals. Besides, who cares if she did have a boyfriend? It's not like you're interested?" Lucifer took another bite of his dog while slyly watching his conflicted minion. It really entertained him to no end to watch Remy fighting his emotions.

"Of course I'm not interested. She's just an assignment."

Lucifer snorted, and a flame shot out, singeing his pickle. "While I appreciate the lying, even I'm not that stupid. You like the girl."

"Maybe. But she hates me."

"And when has that ever stopped you?"

"She's different."

"Really? Funny, she looks like a woman to me. Two legs. A pair of tits. A hole instead of a rod. Slap her with some of your famous sex mojo, fuck her good and clean her out of your system."

Features tight, Remy faced him. "She's more than a hole to fuck. She's smart, and mouthy. Brave too."

"Hmm, them sounds like the words of a man looking for more than a quick screw."

"That's what I'm afraid of."

"Excuse me? A soldier of Hell scared of an itty bitty woman."

Remy's arched brow made Lucifer laugh.

"Okay, she is a force to be reckoned with, but still, it sounds to me like it's the idea of commitment scaring you, boy."

"Not exactly. As tearful as this will make the female population, as shocking and unexpected as it is to me, I think I'm ready to settle down with one lucky lady. And I'm pretty sure it's the witch."

"So what's the problem?"

"Um, the fact she'll probably try to kill me. Actually, she promised to. It's not exactly what I'd call a good start."

"So change her mind. Show her a different side of yourself. The one that isn't sniffing after everything with a pussy. Introduce her to the soldier with dozens of commendations. Let her meet your family." At Remy's dropped jaw, Lucifer wryly amended. "On second thought, skip that part."

"You make it sound easy."

"Sometimes it is."

"How did you win over Mother Earth? You guys are complete opposites and yet you seem to make it work."

Lucifer scowled. "Damnable woman. Don't speak her name. She's liable to show up and ruin my snack. I shouldn't be eating spicy foods before bedtime," he mimed in a high pitched voice. "That's what a bottle full of antacids is for."

"But I got the impression you liked her?"

Lucifer rolled his eyes. "Of course I do. But it doesn't mean we don't have our differences, boy. It's part of what makes our relationship fresh and exciting. I disobey her. She punishes me. I get all bad ass with her, and then chase her around the castle while she giggles and strips."

"Um, too much information, boss."

"No, too much info would be me inviting you to see the home video I made. But, we're getting off topic. Forget about my fabulous sex life, hard I know since I am so wonderful, and let's focus on you, which again goes against the grain, considering Hell revolves around me. Stop acting like a pussy with the witch, and get on with it. You want her. She wants you or she would have turned you into a bug and squashed you. Everything else will work itself out as you go along."

Remy straightened. "You're right. I am a soldier in Hell's army. Nothing defeats me. I shall take an example from the greatest womanizer Hell has known and –"

"Shhh! Are you trying to get me kicked out of bed again? Gaia hates it when people remind her of my reputation."

"You mean that of a man-whore?" The petite form of Mother Earth appeared suddenly, and Lucifer just about fell off his stool.

"Would you knock first?" he exclaimed.

"But then I wouldn't hear you basking in the admiration of all the times you cheated on me," she snapped, green eyes glowing.

"For the millionth time, I didn't even know we were a couple. How convenient of you to forget the spell you used on me. Remember the one that wiped all my memories of you?"

She sniffed. "A man who truly loved me would have still known and not strayed."

"We were on a break!" Lucifer yelled.

"That excuse didn't work for Ross, and it won't work for you," she sassed back.

"Um, I think I should leave." Remy eased off his stool and backed away. Gaia turned her fierce gaze on him, and eyes wide, his demon turned tail and fled.

Laughing Gaia bounced into Lucifer's lap. "That was fun, even if I don't know who that was."

"He's my first attempt at an experiment."

"An experiment in what?" she asked.

"Who cares about work, when I've got something more interesting to show you," he replied with a leer, not ready to divulge his master plan. Lucky for him, she found his hard problem intriguing. And no, he didn't mean his dick. Sick perverts. Although, he did give it to her when he bent her over the newest rock he'd added to the garden as a present for her. Shaped like a penis, it seemed only fitting, especially when she commented on its spectacular size.

8

THE KNOCK at the door made her drop the armful of ice in the tub with a loud clatter. She planned to use the polar bath as a way of soothing her body after the flames died down. It cost her several potions and a curse to get this much ice at one time, given Hell's climate wasn't exactly conducive to ice-making.

Basic mortal things, like refrigerators, tended to work only sporadically or not at all. Some of the blame resided on the power generators for each circle. It took a lot of damned souls to pedal the bikes that spun the turbines to create electricity. If a pandemic took a section out – Hell not being immune to sickness, unfortunately – then brown outs occurred. Less in the Lord's palace of course, given he got prime pick of pedal pushers, but still, a person couldn't always rely on their electronics.

Not that Ysabel minded. She'd grown up in far more primitive conditions. As a matter of fact, she still refused to cave to the modern trend of owning a hellphone or posting a profile on Hellbook. She left that kind of easy accessibility and openness to the younger witches.

Tub full, she stood back to regard the mound of ice. Already the heat of her home fought to melt it. A rap came again at the entrance, more like an impatient pounding, and she cursed. The clock showed her only a few minutes away from her torture.

I need whoever it is to go away.

She ran to the door and slid open the peek-a-boo slot. Familiar turquoise eyes peered back.

"Little witch, little witch, let me come in," he chanted in a gruff voice.

A smile curled her lips. "Not by the wart on my chinny chin chin," she replied. "And before you try huffing and puffing, Nefertiti herself spelled this door. So forget blowing it down."

"So open it then. I've got a lead I think on escapee number three."

A glance at the clock showed one minute left. "Um, I'm kind of in the middle of something. Can you come back in like half an hour?"

"Why not just let me in and I'll wait while you do your thing? I promise not to watch, unless you like an audience."

"I can't. Please. Just go away. I promise I'll let you in when you come back."

His eyes narrowed. "Open this door, Ysabel."

"No. Now go away. I'll talk to you in half an hour." She slammed the slot shut and only allowed herself a moment to lean against the door which shuddered as he hit it with a fist. She didn't have time to deal with his frustration.

The tickle in her toes started and she ran to the bathroom, dropping her robe as she moved. The fire erupted, and standing on the lava tile in her bathroom, she concentrated on breathing against the spiraling pain and flames.

I mustn't scream. Remy might still be there, listening. Why that mattered, she couldn't have said, but it did help her focus for a short moment. But the punishment would not allow her respite. Flames licked up her frame, demolishing her thin underpants and she couldn't help but scream as the agony tore through her body.

Make it stop. Make it stop. Wishing, praying, pleading didn't stop the torture.

As the inferno consumed her, her ears roared with the snap of the fire and a glance in her mirror horrified her, for there she stood – a living pyre of fire. She closed her eyes against the brilliant heat, but that just seemed to amplify the pain.

Her knees buckled, but she didn't fall. Something clasped her and she moaned as she sensed more than saw Remy's arms wrap around her waist. It had to be him. Who else was crazy enough to break down her door and interrupt?

Forcing open her eyes, eyes that wanted to water but couldn't as the heat dried up all moisture, she saw the flames, not picky about their choice of combustion material, as they danced upon his skin. Even caught in her own nightmare, she knew enough to try and push him away with hands that glowed inferno bright.

He wouldn't budge, and he didn't scream – just held her as the curse ran its course.

Without being told, once the flames disappeared, he placed her in the ice bath, the shocking cold a welcome relief. Gasping from the pain, she couldn't speak but remained aware of how he stroked her hair back from her face and how his arm rested around her shoulders, cradling her.

"Oh, my poor little witch," he murmured. "No wonder you've been hiding."

Teeth chattering as the cold penetrated her feverish limbs, she tried to reply. "Wh-what c-c-can I say? I'm h-h-hot."

He didn't laugh and she opened her eyes to see him staring at her with a tight expression. "How long has this been happening? And why?"

"S-s-since the souls es-escaped. And it won't stop until I get them back." As the chill seeped into her body, numbing her enflamed, yet undamaged nerves, she relaxed. "According to my contract, I will suffer the method of my death daily, the time of burning increasing with each day they are loose."

"You burned alive!" It was less a question and more a shocked statement.

"It's what they did to witches back in the day," she said lightly. She shifted in her ice bath, clarity returning quickly now the curse had run its course for the day. It occurred to her at that moment she was naked. Not that Remy seemed to notice. He seemed too intent on her method of death. For some reason it miffed her.

"These souls, they had a hand in your burning?"

"Very much so. Pedro, Emmanuelle, and Alvaro were avid participants."

"And the woman, Luysa and her son, Francisco?"

A sigh escaped her. How much of the truth should she relay? "Luysa was the one who headed the mob and the decision to burn me as a witch. I was involved with her son, and she couldn't handle it. Thought I wasn't good enough for her precious, baby boy."

"You loved him?"

"I did. And I thought he loved me back."

"But?"

Her words emerged low and steely. "He arrived in time to save me. To do something. But he never loved me. It was all lies. He watched me burn." He proved that love didn't matter. That no matter how well she knew a person, she could never truly trust them. People only ever looked out for themselves.

Remy jumped to his feet and paced the small amount of floor in the bathroom. "Fucking son of a bitch. I am going to rip his arm off and beat him with it. I am going to shove hot coals up his –"

"Why are you so mad?" she asked, distracting him with words as she stood from the tub. With her back to him, she reached for her robe. Her fingers never managed to clasp the fabric, as he spun her around and yanked her close. Damp, chilled flesh met the heat of his chest. It sent a shock through her, a pleasurable one. It was then she noticed that while his skin survived the fire, his shirt hadn't. His pants, obviously a more flame retardant material, at least still covered him – how unfortunate. *I'll bet he's a sight to see fully naked.*

Where that surprising idea came from, she didn't know, but once thought, she couldn't deny a curiosity. Just how well-endowed was he?

"Why am I mad?" He seemed surprised by her question. "I'm pissed because this Francisco fellow is a grade A asshole who let his psycho mother torch you to death."

"I still don't get why you care. You didn't know me back then and I've pretty much gotten over it."

"Liar. What he did haunts you still so much that you won't let another man get close to you. You fear commitment."

How did he guess? Or was he fishing? "What are you talking about? I had Felipe over just last night."

"I know that's the name of your cat, just like I know you've not been with a man since your death."

"Lucifer," she growled. Stupid boss, getting involved in her business as usual. "If you give me any frigid or lesbian jokes I'm going to hurt you."

"No jokes. I'm glad you've sworn off men."

Puzzle, her brow creased. "You are. Why?"

"Because five hundred years of celibacy makes you practically a virgin. Untouched and so tempting. It makes the fact you kissed me and want me special."

"I don't want you."

"Such a fibber." He pressed her tighter to him, his hands, big and warm, rubbing over the bare skin of her back.

Despite her adamant stance, he was right. She lied. Her burgeoning arousal, evident by the rock hard nipples digging into his chest, all the proof he needed. But she couldn't let her hormones rule her again. The last time it cost her life.

"I feel nothing for you."

His hands dipped lower and cupped her ass cheeks, hoisting her body until her face was almost level with his.

"What are you doing?" she asked, more breathless than she liked.

"Proving you wrong," he growled, dipping his head. He

kissed her and Ysabel completely forgot why getting this close to Remy was a bad idea. Forgot everything except her need for more.

Her arms twined around his neck, her mouth opened for his tongue and a fire of a different sort, a pleasurable one that burned hotter than her nightmare, swept her body. He kissed her like he wanted to eat her alive. She kissed and nibbled at him, just as hungry.

The cold tile of her vanity distracted her when he seated her on the cool, polished surface. She ignored it as he pushed his thick body between her thighs. The leathery material of his pants provided a soft friction that impeded her from touching him skin to skin. Digging her fingers into the waist band, she tugged him closer, wrapped her legs around his torso and wantonly pressed herself against the hard bulge in his front.

Fingers tangled in her hair, he tilted her back, kissing her with a passion that left her breathless. Sucked at her tongue until she panted and mewled with need. When he pulled back, she keened in loss only to cry out in pleasure as his mouth travelled down the column of her neck and pressed scorching kisses in the deep valley of her breasts.

"So fucking beautiful," he murmured against her skin, rubbing his bristle against her flesh, a teasing touch that made her arch. Her nipples, pointed and aching caught his attention. He plucked one with his lips, teasing the bud, sending coils of heat and desire to her cleft.

Raised in a time where sex was done, but not spoken of, she didn't know what to say, what to beg for other than more. She needed him to ease the tightness inside her. To…

Lips still latched around her nipple, he plunged two

fingers into her channel, and she screamed – a primal sound of pleasure as her body exploded so quick she couldn't catch her breath.

And still he didn't relent, stroking her with his fingers, sucking at her tender flesh until she writhed beneath him again, tilted her hips hard against his hand, begging silently for more.

She heard the sound of a zipper lowering. Felt the hard thickness of him as he slapped his shaft against her wetness. Too far gone to stop things or even coherently remember why she'd thought bedding Remy a bad idea, she waited for him to bring her to climax again.

A roar split through the sounds of their pants.

"What the fuck?" he cried, letting her go to turn and face the beast at her bathroom door.

Sighing, more in disappointment than anything else, Ysabel sat up and peered over his shoulder. She stared down the snarling creature in the doorway. "Meet my cat, Felipe. I should probably mention, he doesn't like strangers.

———

UNDERSTATEMENT OF THE YEAR. THE GIGANTIC, FURRY, striped monster with saber teeth and red glowing eyes was her cat? "Holy fuck, woman. He's the size of a bloody car."

"Shhh," she hissed as she hopped off the vanity and made her way around him to pet the head of the scary beast. "You'll hurt his feelings."

Hurt his fucking feelings? Was she loonier than his mother? No, but she did keep surprising him at every turn.

While she crooned nonsense to the giant hellcat, Remy did his best to buckle his pants, all the while aware of the feline's big bright – not really friendly – eyes watching.

Miffed he'd gotten interrupted, and after she'd come apart so gloriously in his arms, his remark emerged a bit scathing. "Where do you keep the giant furball's litter box? Or have you trained him to use the toilet?"

"Felipe is an outdoor cat who comes and goes as he pleases. Mostly goes when the lady kitties are in heat, don't you, my big furry baby."

Remy rolled his eyes as the creature craned its head for a scratch and began to purr, the sound on par with a lawnmower – missing a muffler, twenty years out of tune. And he could have sworn the damned thing smirked at him as his witch, still naked, rubbed against his fur.

Looking closer, Remy itched to grab his sword, especially as he recognized the intelligence in the hellcat's eyes. This was no ordinary kitty she played with.

"Would you get Felipe a steak from the fridge while I get dressed?" she asked, flouncing off naked, her ass cheeks jiggling. Stunned speechless for a moment, the view truly incredible, he didn't have time to retort before he found himself alone with the cat. A cat who stood and showed him his tail and ass end as it wandered away.

Emerging from the bathroom, he watched it saunter into the kitchen, and Remy stalked after it. "I know you're not a pureblood hellcat. So what's your game? And what do you want with my witch?" he growled in a low voice.

The huge cat shrugged, the gesture so human like, it took him aback.

"Did you find the meat?" Ysabel hollered from the

bedroom. "I had the butcher deliver some this morning because I had a feeling Felipe was going to pop in."

"I got it," Remy snarled as he tore open the fridge and pulled out something bloody wrapped in brown, wax paper. He tossed the hunk of meat at the feline, trying not to wince as the huge jaws opened and snapped shut on its meal. *I guess I should count myself lucky he didn't take a bite of me while I was distracted.* So distracted he never heard a gigantic feline arrive. Pet or not, he already didn't like the creature.

Remy leaned against the counter with his arms crossed. "I'm telling you right now to stay out of my way. She's mine." He staked his claim in a low tone lest his words carry. He didn't need Ysabel freaking out over his caveman announcement. Because if one thing became certain in that bathroom, and before he'd even touched her in a sexual manner, he wanted her.

Holding her as she burned alive, victim to a curse, he'd felt so many things– helpless, afraid, angry. He wanted to hunt the other souls down, right that very minute and bring them back to Hell so she wouldn't hurt anymore. He wanted to ask Crax to let him aid in their punishment, knowing they'd hurt his witch. Hell, he even wanted to take Lucifer to task for putting such a ridiculous clause in her contract to start with.

He and the cat stared each other down, kind of disconcerting considering the giant beast also polished off the raw meat all the while, maintaining his gaze. It licked its chops and Remy snorted. "She has no idea does she? She thinks you're just some plain ol' cat." The damn thing practically laughed at him, chuffing at his statement. "How long have you been hanging out around her?"

"I've had Felipe since he was a baby," she answered, coming into the room wearing jeans and a halter top. "Do you often talk to animals? And of even more interest, do they answer back?"

"Just thinking aloud," he lied. "So you found him as a kitten and took him in. Pretty brave considering his mama can track a flea through a swamp and would kill anyone who touched her kittens."

"His mother was dead. I found him hiding in the brush nearby, half-starved and covered in snake bites. Even though he was just a baby, he was a fighter, weren't you, Felipe?" she crooned scratching his chin again.

Yeah, he couldn't hold back his snort or rolling eyes that time.

"What?" she asked, catching him in the act.

"You do realize he's a three ton killer right?"

"Who would never hurt his mama, would you, baby?" She rubbed her nose against him, and if it weren't for the fact Remy was insanely jealous of her treatment of the creature – who was definitely more than he let on – he would have thought it funny. His witch possessed even more facets than he knew. That of baby talking, crazy cat lady was surprising – and cute.

"Don't call me when he decides to bite your face off one day." He said it but didn't believe it. Much as it disgusted him to admit, Felipe wouldn't hurt the witch. Although, he'd probably tear apart anyone who tried. *I should count myself lucky he didn't tear off a limb when he caught me fooling around with her.*

"I'd be more worried about somebody else losing dangly bits," she replied with a sly smile and a pointed look at his covered groin.

It took a little more fortitude than he liked not to cover his man-parts at her subtle threat, especially when the damned feline bared its teeth. "You know, I liked you a lot more a few minutes ago when you were just moaning, 'Yes! Yes, Remy, you big stud muffin. Give it to me.'"

The blush in her cheeks totally delighted him.

"I said no such thing," she huffed.

"But you thought it," he replied with a wink.

"You caught me during a weak moment. It won't happen again."

"Oh yes it will, but next time, we won't get interrupted." He'd make sure of it by dragging her to his place and locking his door; bars, chains, deadbolt and more if needed.

"But aren't you the one who loves an audience?" And yes, she said it with a straight face.

"Witch." He said it in a warning tone.

She smirked. "What, demon? Not used to your sex dolls talking back?"

"If you weren't hiding behind your cat…"

"You'd what? Take me over your knee and spank me?"

"Yes. Then I'd lick those red cheeks. Then your pussy before I tossed you onto your bed and fucked you."

That threw her for a loop judging by the flare of interest in her eyes and the way she bit her lower lip. "You know what, I'm almost still aroused enough to let you. But, not only will Felipe tear off an important part if you try, we have work to do. This whole daily barbecue thing is getting old real fast."

Way to slap him with reality, however, she was right. He needed to track those souls for her. Save her from the curse. Buy groceries for a month. Block off the kitty's access to the apartment. Then he could put his plan into action, a pleasurable plan that would result in chafing in sensitive places and a smile so silly he'd put clowns to shame.

First though, work. Because he couldn't do a thing until the job was done.

But she is so worth the effort. And the aching blue balls. Sigh...

9

As they travelled to a bar where Remy's source claimed some medieval spirit was harassing the girls, she couldn't help but relive what happened in her bathroom. And she didn't mean the fabulous climax Remy gave her and the second one that got interrupted.

He'd heard her scream, caught her in the midst of her personal nightmare, and he didn't run away or wait it out. He held her. Stayed with her while it ran its course, and though his fire demon status protected him from the flames, she still appreciated the gesture. Most males would have walked away.

As if that weren't astonishing enough, he got angry. She couldn't deny a certain pleasure in hearing him condemn Francisco's and the other's actions, in knowing he wanted vengeance for her death. It made her...like him.

It also made her vulnerable, so that when he kissed her and touched her, she didn't fight. For the first time in five hundred years, she let a man caress her intimately – and she enjoyed it. Wanted to do it again as a matter of fact.

But I can't just throw myself at him like some crazed old witch. Desperate wasn't sexy, even if that was how she felt. Besides, judging by the way she kept catching his eyes on her – filled with male appreciation and a smoldering heat that promised wicked things – it was only a matter of time before he seduced her again. She just needed to exercise some patience.

She also needed to practice reining in a surprising jealousy. As soon as they walked into the strip joint, with naked breasts hanging out everywhere and more cheeks than she could count with dental floss tucked between them, the green eyed monster had her narrowing her gaze. Something in her posture must have given her away.

Tucking her into his side, Remy dipped his head low enough to murmur. "Sheath your claws, my sexy cougar. These slags can't hold a candle to you."

Startled he'd read her so easily, she peeked up at him. He winked. She warmed. And then he ruined the moment. "Of course, I wouldn't be against you getting a glittery thong and dancing around a pole."

"In your dreams, demon."

"You have. And might I say," he crooned in the shell of her ear, "that your finishing move atop my pole is the best I've ever seen."

Shaking her head at his crude, sexual one-liners – and blushing at the backwards compliment – she left his side and strode into the den of iniquity. Talk about a dump.

On the far edge of the ninth circle, where the lowest of the low lived, any attempts at niceties evaporated. The lighting barely illuminated the smoky tavern, which given how her feet stuck to the floor, probably counted as a good thing. The dancers were listless, their bodies all marred by some type of imperfection, from a lopsided set of breasts, to the legless female who swung around on her arms.

Then again, the patrons weren't much better. A more disreputable group she'd never seen, and she'd seen a lot as Lucifer's assistant. The dregs of society seemed to have congregated in this forsaken place – and forgotten to bathe. She made a mental note to have the health inspection unit pay a visit. The dancers deserved better, and as for the men, there were always dirty jobs in need of dispensable crew.

Who cared if the place was a festering plague just waiting to infect? She needed to find Alvaro. It seemed, unlike the previous two souls, he liked his new home in Hell and didn't stray to the mortal side. He also liked to make a nuisance of himself with girls just trying to eke out a living.

Given Lucifer's policy on rape – which he considered on a wholly different level than sexual harassment – word moved quickly about the fellow who thought it was okay to pinch and fondle the girls at work despite their repeated 'No's. He'd even gotten kicked out of a few strip bars before this one.

And judging by the crack that sounded – a well-deserved slap she'd wager – Alvaro was moments away from getting the bum rush once again.

Given her diminutive height, Ysabel didn't manage to see her prey until she landed almost on top of him. A taller demon fellow moved suddenly out of the way and brought her in direct view of Alvaro. His eyes widened in shock, but only for a moment before he grinned, displaying a gap toothed mien, which given the state of decay, made her vow to brush her teeth three times a day.

"Hello, Alvaro."

Unlike her previous two escapees, he didn't engage her in conversation. Waving goodbye, he slid out of his seat and bolted. As if Ysabel would let him get away so easily.

She took off after him, only to stop short when a large body stepped in her path. His size, while incredible, couldn't hold a candle to his rancid stench and hairiness. Holding her breath, she tried to veer around the revolting frame, careful not to touch lest she need to cut off her hand to prevent infection, but the idiot in her path jiggled from side to side matching and blocking her attempts to get around.

"Would you move out of my way?" she snapped, glaring up at the brutish male who seemed determined to thwart her.

"You're new," the guy possessed of trollish ancestry, or so she assumed given his green hue, flat nose and tusks, stated. "Show me what you got."

"I'm not a dancer."

"Don't care. You're pretty. I like pretty things," he rumbled reaching out a paw to grab her.

She evaded his grip, but it didn't stop him from swiping at her again. The things she had to put up with because she owned two breasts. *Time to show him to respect the ladies.* She chanted under her breath, and waggled her fingers. The massive male in front of her shrank, and shrank, then diminished in size some more until he stood waist high. She crouched in front of him with a smirk.

"Next time a witch tells you to move, don't talk back."

"Bitch!" he yelled.

She wiggled her fingers again and he squeaked before running off. But her fiasco with the troll had cost her precious time. Alvaro had fled. He also wasn't the only one missing.

Just where did my demon guard go? Remy had also disappeared. *He'd better not have gone off somewhere private with one of those sluts.* Not that she cared. Really. A claim that screamed 'Lie' with every stomp she took as she exited the bar.

Hands on her hips she peered up and down the refuse lined street. "Stupid, good for nothing, testosterone laden…"

"You called?" Remy's query came from behind her.

Whirling, she meant to glare at him, but instead gasped, "You caught him!"

He sure had. Hanging from Remy's grasp, looking none too happy, was one village drunk named Alvaro. Back in the day, he'd claimed, to all who would listen, that he'd seen her flying her broom and dancing naked around fires. The fact he was a drunken wastrel who barely remembered his own name let alone recalled what happened five minutes previous didn't matter to the people anxious to condemn her. It just added fuel to the charges against her.

Funny thing though, was the things he accused her of were true. He'd just never actually witnessed them.

"Of course I caught him. While you were busy playing

with the patrons and taunting them with what they couldn't have, I was out earning a kiss."

"Only a kiss?" she teased, immeasurable happy for some reason that he'd not found a dark corner to screw a slut but instead, kept to their task. And now he wanted a reward, *from me!*

"Dammit. I knew I should have held out for more."

"Argh. Someone get me some ale. The pair of you are making me sick."

"Shut it," they both told Alvaro at the same time. Pulling out her tag, she slapped it on his body and waved good bye as he got sucked back to prison.

"I'm surprised you didn't keep him to question."

She shrugged. "Why bother? If he's like the last two, we won't learn anything. Besides, I believe I owe you a kiss." Did those wanton words come from her? They did, but she didn't need to worry if he thought her presumptuous because she no sooner spoke than Remy scooped her into his arms and plastered his lips over hers.

Just as toe curling as before, his embrace woke her body, roused her need. She clung to him, tasted him and hungered.

"Hey mate. Mind passing her along when you're done?"

As rude interruptions went, it ranked high, but the fist Remy put in the idiot's face, sending him flying proved beyond delightful. She laughed, a soft sound at first that grew as he growled in the direction of the crowd of thugs gathered to watch them.

"I fail to see the humor," he muttered as he beckoned those waiting with crooked fingers.

"It's just, he said the kind of thing I've come to expect

from you. So I find it funny that you would get so mad about it."

He turned his head and hit her with the full force of his stare. "When it comes to you, my little cougar, I won't share. You belong to me. And I want everyone in Hell to know it."

The declaration, blood thirsty and unexpected, left her speechless – and even more aroused than before, a heat that rose with each thug he took down. With flashing fists, well aimed kicks and a savage grace that made her cheer, he eradicated the fiends who thought to attack him and then take her. Not that it would have happened. She had more than enough magic to send them crying, but the gallant gesture, one she'd never experienced before, at least not aimed at her, made her happy. More than happy, she discovered in that moment, she liked Remy. Really, really liked him. Was perhaps even falling in love.

It should have sent her screaming. Or made her turn him into a fire-lizard. Instead, as soon as he was done wiping the ground with his assailants, she threw morals and caution to the wind, jumping into his arms and laying the kiss of all kisses on him.

OF ALL THE PLACES SHE COULD HAVE DECIDED TO SEDUCE him, she chose the worst, Remy thought, not that he stopped her. On the contrary, he let Ysabel wrap herself around his body and with one eye on the shadows and the threat they might contain, he carried her to the nearest portal and in no time had them back in the primary ring, outside of the castle.

All the while, they kissed. Even groped a little. Hot, hard and hungry for her, he didn't dare let her up for air lest she change her mind. Besides, it wasn't as if he could have stopped. His need for her seemed bottomless, and despite the odd looks they garnered on their trek – stares he caught and, with a rude gesture, halted – he didn't stop, nor did he let himself think about what it meant. What she meant to him. He did know that his earlier claim that she belonged to him felt right. As did his fight to take down the unworthy bastards who thought to fantasize about his witch. *My witch. And no one gets to think about her doing the naughty but me. With me.*

A part of him should have panicked at the possessive feeling she evoked. Ran screaming into the wilds at how she seemed to consume every part of him, from his body, to his heart, and what he owned of his soul – Lucifer, as Lord of this domain, owned the rest. Instead of looking for ways to leave without a trace, though, a fierce joy possessed him. He didn't understand it, but he embraced it, and let her feel his inexplicable happiness in his kiss and touch. But seriously, he needed to find them a private spot or else he'd end up doing something crazy like fucking her in public, and while necking could pass muster, he somehow doubted the actual act would. And what she thought, what she experienced their first time together, mattered. *That and I'd prefer to not have her kill me.* Not to mention, the things he wanted to do to her... Yeah, he wanted no one to see her naked, sighing and squirming but him.

So he needed to find a room, which presented a dilemma. Where to go?

He vetoed her apartment because he didn't fancy any

interruptions – or chewed off body parts – from her damned cat. Which left him his place, well, more like his room. He'd never gotten around to really getting his own apartment given his assignments sent him all over the place. Most nights, he slept in some lucky female's bed, and when he took a night off, he boarded in a barrack.

When working close to the castle, and in between girlfriends, he tended to live at home. Call him a momma's boy and he'd pull your intestines out of your belly button and make you siphon them like spaghetti. But, really, he did enjoy the perks of home life from the laundry and mending, to the home cooked meals. Sure, he occasionally had to deal with some inconveniences like when his mother covered all the windows, got rid of all the lights and candles so the imps couldn't find and steal her smuggled Oreo cookies. But the paranoia wasn't her fault. He had a weakness for the sugary sweet centers, not that he admitted his culpability. She'd shaved him bald while he slept the last time she caught him stealing her treats.

But Mom left on that holiday to the beach, so no worries about her barging in and saying something embarrassing. Or crazy. Part fire demon, a whole lot of nuts, and the one who raised him, his mother took getting used to. Although, most of the time she acted as a great deterrent to overeager females who wanted to get their claws in him. Great usually, except he didn't want Ysabel to run far, far away. *But if I intend to keep her, which seems more and more likely, she'll eventually have to meet Mom.*

Oh, shuddering fucking hell. Now there was a bridge he'd cross tomorrow, or maybe in a decade. Yeah, the longer he kept the pair apart, the better. And he really needed to stop thinking of his mom because his witch nipped him hard, sensing his distraction.

How remiss of him. He hugged her tight to let her know he'd not forgotten and let his tongue ply hers with sensual caresses that soon had her moaning deliciously again.

Tonight, or what was left of it, he intended to take full advantage of his witch's passion. Hopefully, he'd make it memorable enough she wouldn't kill him in the morning – or make fun of him for still living with his parents.

Thankfully, his family home wasn't too far from the portal, and he staggered there, drunk on kisses, letting himself in via an old fashioned manner when he realized he'd have to let her go if he wanted to grab his key. Fuck that. He kicked the door in, an impatient act that earned him breathy giggles that made his rope of patience snap.

Using his booted foot, he managed to slam the door shut, kind of. It no longer wanted to latch, but at least they were out of view. And best of all, alone.

Pressing her up against the wall, he tore at her blouse, ripping buttons off in his haste. Her creamy breasts appeared encased in black lace, the tops of them spilling over. He buried his face in that sweet valley while she clutched at his hair.

"I can't wait," he groaned. "I'm sorry. I need you so fucking bad."

"Do it," she urged. "Before I change my mind and remember why this is a bad idea."

Oh no she wouldn't. Seams ripped, fabric parted in record time as he bared her from the waist down. But, he left her sexy heels on.

Cupping her pussy, he growled in pleasure at the heat

and moisture he found. How he longed to taste it. But he also wanted to sink into her. Dammit. What was a poor demon to do?

Show a little restraint and finesse.

Dropping to his knees, she clasped his hair and gasped as he nuzzled her mound. She didn't stop him when he pushed at her thighs, parting them. The scent of her arousal, a heady aroma that made his head swim, also made his mouth water. His first lick, a slow, long swipe of his tongue, had her shuddering and sighing his name. Again, he licked her, tasting her honey, feeling the quiver of her flesh, the biting dig of her nails in his scalp. The tip of his tongue flicked rapidly, back and forth against her clit, stroking her nub, heightening her pleasure until she keened and squirmed. But he drew back before letting her climax because he wanted to feel her coming on his cock, would die, probably, if he didn't soon ease the pressure building inside him since they met.

Standing, he kept one hand on her sex, lightly stroking her to keep her at a fevered pitch. Her breathing, fast and furious, she regarded him with a heavy lidded passion that brought forth a possessive growl. *Mine.* He couldn't free his shaft fast enough.

Palming her full ass cheeks, he lifted her as he caught her lips for a kiss. She didn't seem to mind the taste of herself on his tongue, the same honey that rubbed along his cock as he slid it under her sex, teasing them both. Her legs wrapped around his waist, loosely though which gave him room to juggle her into position so that the head of his cock came to rest at the entrance of her sex.

He paused before plunging, hesitating because for some reason he knew he stood on the brink of a life changing moment. *Once I claim her with my body, that's it. There will be no other women for me.* He didn't question where this certainty came from. He just knew it to be true.

It didn't stop him.

He pressed the head of his shaft into her. Scalding and moist, he panted as her tight channel gripped him and forced him to penetrate her with a slowness that was both excruciating and damned wonderful. Inch by inch, he made his way into her sex, pushing at the flesh that was tense with excitement. It took a pleasurable eternity before he was fully sheathed, her pussy quivering all around him. Adjusting his grip so that he held her by both thighs with her back flat against the wall, he rotated his hips, driving deeper into her. Her fingers clawed at his shoulders and she bit his lip as he gyrated again, finding her sweet spot and stimulating it. She mewled, a sound that sent shivers to wrack his body as he sensed her need. A need he would fulfill.

Slowly, despite his raging desire to thrust hard and fast, with restraint and a precision that made his body gleam with sweat, he swirled and pressed, never retreating far from her flesh but instead rubbing it, grinding into her.

Talk about agony as he held back. Talk about iron control as her body grew tighter and tighter, squeezing his cock almost painfully. And then, with a loud cry, she came apart. Her climax pulsed, undulating waves of heat and moisture that suctioned his shaft, as he finally allowed himself to lose control and thrust into her. The trembling wave tumbled into a second strangling spasm

EVE LANGLAIS

that made him yell her name as he jetted into her. And still the pleasure kept coming.

He caught her lips and kissed her as he kept his hips thrusting, milking every last ounce of bliss from the moment.

Intense, Hell shattering, body weakening, and more. She leaned her head into the crook his shoulder, her breathing erratic and hot on his skin. He didn't own words grand enough for expressing how he felt. So he said the next best thing as he rubbed his face across her silky crown. "Wow."

HEAD CRADLED AGAINST HIS SHOULDER, HER BODY STILL trembling with aftershocks, Ysabel raised her head to look at Remy. "Did you just say *wow*?"

"Yup."

A giggle escaped her. "That's all you have to say? What's wrong, demon? Run out of suave lines?"

"I don't have anything that seems appropriate."

"So, was it everything you hoped for?" she teased. The light banter surprised her, but not willing to end the moment, she allowed it.

"Oh my little witch, it was so much better than I imagined."

"Really?" Okay that soft, wistful query surely didn't come from her? What did she care if he liked it or not? She was just planning to use him for sex.

"Is this your way of making me show you again? Because I am totally good with that. And this time, maybe we'll even make it to a bed."

She laughed. "That was kind of impatient of us. I'm sorry, I don't usually do crazy things like that."

"As long as you only do them for me," he replied letting her slide down his body until she stood, clad in only her shoes.

"Why would you care? I thought your motto was fuck 'em and leave 'em.'"

"Maybe I'm ready for something different."

He looked so serious that for a moment, she couldn't stop her heart from hammering. She mentally slapped herself. What else did she expect him to say? He wanted to have sex again. Of course he wasn't going to say that she meant nothing to him but a pussy to fuck.

"You don't know how to be serious," she said lightly, fighting to not let sadness enter her tone. No strings sex. It was what she wanted. Nothing else. What she couldn't figure out was why she kept needing to remind herself?

"Oh, you'd be surprised, my sexy cougar. Now what do you say, you get your sweet cheeks up those stairs."

"And what will you be doing?"

A leer and twinkle in his eyes made her quiver. "Why chasing you, of course, while admiring that wicked ass of yours. And imagining what I am going to do to it in a moment."

Her usual bitchy and practical self would have sneered at his suggestion and stalked off to get some sleep so she could get to work tracking down the last two souls. But she'd spent five hundred years living in a cold, emotionless vacuum. For just one day, actually more like early morning, she wanted to let loose. Enjoy. Remember what it felt like to smile and laugh. To feel pleasure.

Bending over to grab her torn blouse and slacks first,

an act that made him groan, she tossed a coy look over her shoulder before bolting up the winding staircase. She only made it to the first landing before he swept her up – to her delighted giggles – and over his shoulder, running the rest of the way to his room. And there, he showed her how much he liked her ass. Breasts. Pussy. Actually, he worshipped every part of her body, making her come so many times she ended up falling asleep, exhausted in his arms, happier that she'd ever been. Wishing it never had to end.

———

WATCHING HER SLEEP IN HIS ARMS HUMBLED REMY BECAUSE whether she'd admit it or not, his prickly witch trusted him. He knew she didn't let people get close to her – and had major issues with men. But she'd overcome her dislike enough to let him into her life, to let him make love to her, and now hold her while she slumbered at her most vulnerable.

Forget denying it. Or pretending it was something else. Remy was in love, however, that knowledge brought a whole wealth of problems and emotions. He needed to protect her, not just from the souls, but those who thought to harm her, and that included Ysabel, herself. Becoming her mate would not happen easily. She would fight him tooth and nail, and with good reason. His reputation in this case would hamper his efforts.

How to make her believe him when he tried to explained he wanted her forever as his mate? How to make her understand that once he gave himself to her, he would never stray? Never hurt her?

She was more likely to lob his head off with magic before she believed him. But he had to try. And it started right now.

Easing out of bed, he dressed quietly and let himself out of the house. There was something he needed to do before she woke up. *My first step into winning her heart.* Hopefully she wouldn't kill him when she found out.

10

Stretching, in a strange bed, sated and smiling, Ysabel couldn't recall ever waking so...what the heck did she feel? Sore, in a pleasant way. Content, like the cat who ate a pet bird. In other words, happy. But more than that, her heart wanted to burst. She felt an urge to sing. Grin. And she possessed a desire to see and thank, in a naked, carnal fashion, one very special demon.

Holy freaking Satan. She was in love. How had that happened?

When did one obnoxious, foul mouthed, good looking and kind hunk manage to get under her prickly shields and ensnare her heart? She didn't know the answer, but somehow, he'd done the impossible. He'd made her feel again. Shown her she'd not lost her capacity to love. Only one problem though. As an undisputed womanizer, their relationship was temporary.

Talk about ruining her high. Despite his declarations, his actions, even her own feelings, she knew better than to think they had a future. Hell's number one panty dropper would never settle down with her. So what could she do?

End things now before they went any farther. Cut herself off from further pleasure at his hands – and tongue.

No. Not so quickly, not when she'd just rediscovered happiness. But the other option, heartache when he eventually moved on…how could she handle it?

There was an option. Kill him. Kill him before he broke her heart, then she could at least live with the happy memories instead of watching them get twisted with hatred as happened with her previous lover. However, that did seem a little drastic.

I'm a five hundred year old witch. Other women deal with breakups, surely I can too. Like she had with Francisco? But in that case she had ample reason for anger given he let her burn alive. She knew Remy would never do anything like that. Despite his tough guy attitude and exterior, he wouldn't intentionally hurt her.

It's not his fault my stupid heart fell in love.

Or maybe she was totally misreading things. As the first male she'd had sex with in five hundred years, it didn't automatically mean the Big L. Maybe she was just horny. Perhaps her good will toward him owed more to the fact he scratched her sexual itch.

Yeah. She could deal with that. Use him for sex until she tired of him. Given she'd gone centuries without a male between her legs, surely it wouldn't take long to sate her new need. She'd stay in his bed and use his body. And if things ended before she'd quite managed to slake her lust, then she'd pay a visit to Francisco and his friends.

Torture them a little. That would surely raise her spirits – and remind her why men were scum.

Decided, she sat up in the ridiculously large bed and peered around. Of her big demon stud, she saw no sign. Odd because she'd felt him kiss her bare shoulder before he slipped out of bed a while back. He'd just never returned.

I suppose it's too much to hope he's gone to find us some coffee. And a donut. Don't judge. She figured burning at the stake entitled her to the sweet treats.

Gaze roving around his room done up in a masculine grey, brown and blue with no velvet or silk sheets in sight, she caught a glimpse of a clock – a silhouette of a woman's naked body –and gasped.

They'd slept late. Too late. Less than fifteen minutes remained before the curse hit.

"Shit! Damn! Fuck!" She cursed as she hopped out of his bed and scrambled around looking for clothes. It didn't even occur to her to stay in his room for her fiery act. She wanted the comfort of her home, her space when it happened. She also wouldn't have minded Remy's arms, and that simple thought halted her frenzied actions.

The man who held me all night long, and caressed me with such passion wouldn't leave me alone with the hour of my death approaching unless he had very good cause. Or so she hoped. For some reason it was important to her that he not turn out to be a jerk like most males she'd encountered. But if she believed he wouldn't leave her alone for her daily brush with fire, then where was he? Did he simply linger elsewhere in what appeared from the outside as a huge manor? If she left would she miss him as he returned to her?

Indecision didn't sit well with her, and neither did bursting into flame in an unknown place. He'd know where to find her if he wanted to, and she was a big girl. So what if today's torture would last one more hellish minute? Her original death lasted an eternity in her agonized mind, and yet she survived, of a sorts.

Locating the tattered remains of her ruined clothes – a reminder of their impatience and passion the night before – she ditched them in favor of something more functional. She pulled on a shirt of his that she located hanging over a chair, biting her lip against the soft pleasure that wanted to relax her as his scent enveloped her.

Slipping her feet in to her shoes, which survived somehow despite their frantic trek to his bed – and the episode where he pounded into her missionary style while she dug the heels into his back – she bent over to buckle the clasps only to hear an amused feminine voice say, "Did panties go out of style while I vacationed?"

Whipping upright, Ysabel regarded the stranger who'd entered. Tall, with a shapely figure, red hued skin, bright yellow eyes, and a pair of horns projecting from her ash blonde hair, the older woman arched a brow at Ysabel's perusal. Then shocked the wits of out her when she reached under her voluminous skirts and emerged with a bright purple pair of underpants.

Flinging them to the side, the obviously deranged woman grinned. "That's better. I won't have it said that I'm not sticking with current trends."

Blinking in shock, it took Ysabel a moment to speak. "I'm sorry. But who are you?"

"I'm the mother of the boy you screwed last night."

"Mother?" Ysabel almost choked on the word. Great.

Just great. Caught by Remy's mama. Exactly how to handle this? The last mother she'd interacted with didn't handle her involvement with her son very well. How would this one react?

"Yes. I'm that darling boy's mother. Took me three days to birth his fat head. You should keep that in mind when you decide to get pregnant. My poor cunny was never the same after."

"Pregnant?" she squeaked. Ysabel sat down hard on the edge of the bed. "No. I'm afraid you have this wrong. Remy and I aren't together. And I am most definitely not going to get pregnant with his child." Or so she hoped. She'd completely forgotten to take any precautions the previous night. The realization made her head swim.

"I thought Lucifer banned birth control? Sentimental guy he is, all about family. And rebuilding his army."

"Not with a child of my loins he's not," she retorted.

"Don't be so hasty to speak. I know you had sex. I can smell it all over you and this room. With my son I might add. Which, if his swimmers are anything like his father's, would make him the daddy, unless you let him finish off inside another body part?"

Oh, she so wasn't having this conversation. "I think I should go."

Remy's mother flung her arms across the doorframe, blocking the way out. "No. You can't leave. We've not finished bonding!"

"I'm really confused." And she was. What was up with his mother and her crazy act? Perhaps it was a ploy to get rid of her before Remy returned. In that case, she'd happily oblige before things got even stranger.

"Confused? So am I most of the time." The matron

grinned showing off sharp teeth. "But, my first shrink said it's just because I take things too literally. Of course, I thought he meant that as an insult, and now feel kind of bad in retrospect for taking his head off and kicking it around his office. However, my second shrink, who's much better at explaining things, says I can forgive myself, because of my insanity."

"I see," Ysabel replied faintly, still bewildered and now really worried.

"So, when's the wedding? Or are you going to live in sin? I know Lucifer would love that. My baby boy finally involved in a serious relationship. And it didn't even take Hell freezing over again for it to happen."

Married? "Oh, no. We're not a couple." At the matron's pointed look, Ysabel actually blushed. "Well, we kind of are, but it's just because we're working together. Once we capture some missing souls, our job will be done and Remy will probably move on to the next lucky girl." Who might end up missing a few toes – among other body parts – as Ysabel consoled herself over the loss.

"Denial! I love it. Reminds me of when I met dear old Jacko. It took him tying me to a bed and sexually torturing me for days before I'd admit I cared for him. And he hardly misses the finger I bit off at all. Best days of my life."

Did Remy's mother not grasp the concept of too much information? "I am not in denial. Remy and I aren't settling down together and we're not a couple. It was just sex. You're his mother. You know he beds a different girl just about every night."

A cunning look came into her eyes. "Yes. But he never brings them home."

"What?" There came that lightheadedness again.

"My Remy is a lady's man. Cute bugger gets that from his human father. A dear man that one, but so fragile. What a shame. At least he died with a smile on his face. But I'm getting off track. As I was saying, Remy might fornicate like a bunny on Viagra, but he never, ever brings girls home. The only time I meet his slags is when he invites me to lunch and gets me to scare off the clingy ones. So, the fact you're here, in his bedroom, must mean you're special."

"I'm getting a headache." Bending her head, Ysabel clutched at her skull, the conversation so completely nuts, she didn't even know how to respond anymore. One thing though kept repeating in her head. *I'm the first girl he's brought home?* Surely not. And what did it mean? Nothing. Something. Oh, thinking about it just made the turmoil in her mind worse. And time wasted.

Oh no. Jumping up, she scanned the clock and her breath left in a whoosh. It was time for her torture. She peeked down at her toes to see them intact. Wiggled them, but didn't feel a tingle. Could the clock be wrong?

"Excuse me, what time –"

"What's burning? Do you smell that?" Whipping around, Remy's mother barreled out the door, and unease gripping her, Ysabel followed. Down she went, feet clattering on staircases that wound and ended in blanks walls, forcing her to hop over the railing to where they started again. She barely kept the older female demon in sight as she raced, skirts billowing until they entered a cavern, heavy with smoke and filled with a familiar stench of burning flesh.

It took Ysabel a moment to grasp the situation, to

recognize the burning pyre. Remy's mother understood right away.

"My baby's on fire!" she screamed.

And so he was. Every inch of Remy danced with flames, but he should have been immune. He was part fire demon, however, despite his heritage, she could see the agony by the rictus on his face and the way he clamped his lips tight. He didn't let out a sound, but she could recognize the pain in the way he held himself, and as realization struck her, she sank to her knees with a whispered, "No. Oh no. Why, Remy? Why?"

As fantastical as it seemed, he'd taken over her punishment, and she knew who to blame for that.

LUCIFER WHISTLED AS HE SIGNED OFF ON A BUNCH OF sell-my-soul-for-riches requests. Business boomed. People damned themselves by the thousands. His golf game had vastly improved, meaning his match later that week with his brother stood a chance. Especially if he cheated.

Nothing could bring him down. He was on top of his world.

"I demand you give me back my curse!" yelled a witch who really needed a man to teach her some manners.

Putting his quill down, he tented his fingers. "Can't. Remy bought it fair and square. One hundred years of service in my army. Iron clad agreement signed in blood."

"Rip it up."

Peering at her as she stood before him dressed in a man's shirt that hit her about mid-thigh, her hair tousled and lips swollen, Lucifer grinned. "I see someone got lucky."

"Yes, I had sex. It was great. Can we get back the point? I want you to cancel the contract. Give me back my curse."

"Why would I do that? Shouldn't you be happy you're not going to suffer anymore? I thought he was crazy myself taking it on, especially knowing he wouldn't have his usual fire demon protection to ease the pain. But, you must have done him good." Lucifer wiggled his brows, but Ysabel, lacking a sense of humor, scowled.

"It's my curse. I'm the one who should suffer. Not him."

"Too late. But, really, if it upsets you that much, just find the last two missing souls. Once they're vanquished back to the pit, loverboy stops smelling like roasted venison each day, and our contract with each other will be done."

"It stops when I find Francisco and his mother?"

"Unless you want to make a deal to extend it. I do recall someone not long ago declaring how much she hated a certain demon. Am I to understand, by your current attire, you've changed your mind?"

"No. He's still a rotten pig, but he doesn't deserve to suffer for my mistakes. I'll fetch you those souls. But that's it after that. You and I are done."

"I've got a cake already pre-ordered to celebrate the event, and a pool of ladies dying to take over your position. Have I mentioned the new dress code requires them to be pantyless?"

"Pig."

"I prefer king of seduction."

"Oh really?"

Oh shit. Lucifer pasted a smile on his face as Gaia once again materialized out of nowhere, foot tapping and arms crossed. "My dearest lady, there you are."

"Don't you *my lady* me, you adulterous dog."

"Can we discuss this later? I was having an important discussion with my assistant."

Ysabel narrowed her gaze. "Are you going to release Remy from the curse?"

"No."

Lips tight Ysabel turned to Gaia. "I've got a video of him grabbing the mail girl's ass."

Before Lucifer could explode at Ysabel for tattling, Gaia rounded on him. Judging by the green sparks in her eyes, he'd once again landed in major doo-doo.

Dammit, and I just got off the bloody couch.

11

REMY CAUGHT Ysabel coming out of Lucifer's office. She didn't look pleased. As a matter of fact, her scowl deepened when she caught sight of him. Uh-oh.

"What were you thinking, taking on my curse like that?" she yelled.

"I couldn't stand to see you suffer," he admitted. Most women would have swooned at this comment. His witch? She slugged him in the gut.

"You had no right. It's my burden to bear. Not yours."

"It's not a big deal. We'll catch the two remaining souls, and it will stop. Easy as eating your pie." But not as much fun. He'd only suffered her curse for a few measly minutes and he was already determined to not go through it again, however, he would keep it forever if it kept her from suffering.

"This isn't funny," she growled. "What if we can't find the missing souls? The burning increases by a minute each day."

"You're worried? I knew you liked me."

"No I don't."

"You know, that would be a lot more believable if I didn't have your claw marks embedded in my shoulders still."

A blush was his reward, but it still didn't wipe the worry from her eyes.

"Remy, please stop joking for a minute. Don't you understand how grave this is? The pain will drive you insane if we can't stop it."

Madness? Bah, he dealt with it every day. He shrugged. "I heard you met my mother. I know all about insanity. It's not that bad once you beat up everyone who teases you about it."

"Can't you ever take anything seriously?"

"I do," he said, instantly sober. He pulled her into his arms, relieved she didn't fight him. "I take you very seriously. And I meant what I said. I can't stand to see you suffer. I gladly took on your curse. I would do more to keep you protected from harm."

"But why? I don't understand." Her voice trembled as she asked in a low, husky whisper. Funny how his time with her and the disclosure of her story made him understand her better. He now knew the bitter façade she presented to the world was a cover to hide the pain and loneliness. A self-imposed exile because she feared to trust. Yet, he'd seen enough of her happiness last night when they played to see how she longed for it. Needed it. *And I will give it to her.*

He cupped her face and tilted her so she could see him as he spoke. He caught her gaze and hoped she could read what he felt. See his sincerity. "I care for you, Ysabel."

She shook her head, or tried to. He wouldn't let her

budge. Falling in love, becoming vulnerable to someone again, terrified her. Tears rolled down her cheeks, a weakness she surely hated. "No you don't. We had great sex. That's it. When this is over, another pretty girl will catch your eye and you'll wander off."

"I won't."

"Don't lie to me," she cried, pulling free. "You will. You're just like him. Fucking anything that moves. Telling me pretty lies to get between my legs. You can stop now. I don't believe it. I don't believe you."

"Ysabel. No, it's not like that. Listen to me."

But his witch fled as the choked sound of her sobs reached him. Crushed him. All he'd wanted to do was take away her pain, and show her happiness. Instead, by caring for her, he'd caused her even more anguish. There had to be a way to fix this. To make her believe him.

To make her love me.

Because, despite what she thought, his demonizing days were done. He'd done the craziest thing imaginable. He'd fallen in love with a witch.

YSABEL RAN TO HER SUITE OF ROOMS, UPSET, ANGRY, AND IN fucking love. So much for trying to fool herself earlier that all she felt for Remy was lust. It was love. Stupid, rotten, stinking love.

And for a confirmed manwhore. Didn't that just beat it all? Five hundred years she'd spent hating men and swearing to never let one hurt her again. And what did she do? Fall in love with a demon who kept doing things to soften her up. Who didn't even have to try that hard to make her love him.

The jerk. A jerk she didn't understand.

He'd gotten what he wanted. They'd gone at it like a succubus after a meal of oysters, indulging in hours of sensual pleasure, laughter and even talk. Who would have thought he hid a brain behind the pretty face?

A fun time was had by all. He managed to get her, despite all her claims to the contrary, to have sex, so why continue the charade?

Why would he take on my curse? Why would he put himself through that agony? Because she didn't believe for a minute that he cared for her. Allowing herself to believe was foolish because when it turned out to be false, it would hurt so much. *And I won't allow it.*

Making it to her suite of rooms, she slammed the door shut and activated the binding spells. She wanted no interruptions. No sexy demon barging his way in, tearing down the walls she'd built to protect herself.

I need him out of my life before I fall any further. In order for that to happen, she needed to find Francisco and his mother. Needed to send them to hell, break the curse and get Remy out of her life for good.

The door splintered as something hit it and Remy stalked in, six foot something of male arrogance and hotness.

Not again. Was there not a door in all of Hell that could withstand him?

"What the hell do you think you're doing?" She planted herself in front of him, hands on her hips.

"I've decided that since acting like a wimp and talking

about my feelings didn't work, I'm going to take a page from my stepdad's book."

Ysabel took a step back as he stalked toward her, his bristling maleness arousing. No. This had to stop. No matter how hot he appeared, she couldn't let herself get distracted.

"I'll sic Felipe on you if you lay a hand on me."

"Good luck with that. I saw him through a window in the garden stalking a giant rodent."

"I'll turn you into a toad?" She held her hand up menacingly.

He smirked. "Go ahead, but keep in mind when I shuck the enchantment, I am going to be even more determined."

"Why are you doing this? I don't want you. Is that the problem? Is your ego so big you can't handle a woman rejecting you?"

"Oh, you want me alright, my sexy little witch. Want me so bad it scares you. Well, I've got news for you. It scares the fuck out of me, too. But I don't care. When the options are settling down with you for life and popping out little demonlings or watching you walk away, I know what I choose."

For a moment, she couldn't answer, could only gape at him as his words penetrated. Surely, she misunderstood. "What did you say?"

"I want you as my mate."

No misunderstanding that time. She tamped down her elation by slapping it with the cold, hard truth. "You'll hurt me."

"Trust me."

He asked too much. "I'm not the right woman."

"You're all I want."

She shook her head lest his words weave a spell around her and make her believe. Yet despite all the warnings in her head, hope blossomed and love warmed her. How nice it would be to allow herself to love him. To trust him.

Sadness entered his expression at her rejection. "I know it's hard for you, little witch, but I promise you've nothing to fear. Unless the thought of too many orgasms in a row freaks you out." And that quickly, he changed from pensive male to the one she'd grown to love with the mischievous smile.

He lunged. She squealed like a little girl and ran. Not far though.

With his ridiculously long stride, he quickly caught her and tossed her over his shoulder. He laughed as she beat at his broad back with her fists. "Save some of that energy for the bedroom because you are not leaving until you admit you care for me."

"I'll kill you first."

"I like a girl who's kinky."

"You're impossible."

"No, but I am horny."

"How are we supposed to catch those souls if we're fooling around here?"

"Some things are more important."

"How can having sex with me be more important than ensuring you don't burst into flame tomorrow?"

"I would let someone beat me with a cat-o-nine too, if you'd just admit you like me."

"I hate you."

"Close. I see we'll need to work on that."

EVE LANGLAIS

Flipping her off his shoulder onto the bed, he quickly stripped out of his clothes and covered her frame with his own, pinning her to the mattress. It didn't stop her from bucking and pushing at him. He didn't budge, but he did clasp her hands in one of his fists and pull them above her head.

"Will you admit you like me?"

She glared, keeping her lips clamped tight less she inadvertently blurted out she loved him.

"Such a stubborn witch. I guess we're going to do this the fun way."

Oh no. She couldn't let him have his sensual way. She'd melt under his determined touch and admit her affection, and then she'd end up screwed. *I can't give him the power to hurt me.* Yet, what could she do to stop him? *Cast a spell on him? Call my cat to eat him?* A variety of things she could try ran through her mind, but she didn't attempt any of them. Not with her heart racing, her pussy throbbing, and a part of her hoping, wistfully, that he meant what he said. It seemed his family's insanity was contagious because she didn't put up a fight at all as he set about seducing her.

He kissed her, while one hand fumbled at the hem of her shirt. His shirt. She'd not even stopped to change when she'd charged out of his home and headed straight to Lucifer's office. Worry for him overrode any modesty she owned.

Up went the fabric, inch by inch, baring her flesh to his gaze. He stopped below her breasts as the fabric caught under her back. Anticipation held her breath. He didn't shred the shirt like she expected at this snag, oh no, instead he dipped his head and placed his mouth over her fabric covered breast. The decadent heat of it arched her back and he took advantage, shimmying the shirt over her breasts, a slow ascent that proved maddening. And even worse, he left the top bunched around her arms and tucked under her head, so that when his mouth left hers and began to blaze a trail down her torso, she couldn't even reach to touch him. To pull him closer. Not that the hand still gripping her wrists released her.

He held her pinned and exposed to his ardent gaze, and stare at her he did, the smoldering look raising her nipples into hard points while her sex warmed. Unbidden, she spread her legs to accommodate his body. But he didn't place himself atop her like she wanted. Didn't press himself against her core and rub where she ached.

Frustrated, and eager, she arched – hips, breasts, anything to try and connect with his body. He remained out of reach and she couldn't stop a growl of impatience. It made him chuckle.

"Tell me, little witch."

"Either fuck me or let me go," she demanded, not ready to admit anything, but too aroused to not ask for more.

"Such language. I like it," he said with a twinkle in his eyes. He pulled her arms down and held them fisted under her breasts as he shuffled lower. "I am never letting you go, my impatient cougar. And as for making love to your delectable body, I'll do that, but not until you tell me what I want." He murmured the last part against her rounded tummy.

Rubbing his face, and the rough growth of hair he'd not shaved that morn, he kissed his way down to her thigh, his breath tickling her skin and making her hips arch. He blew on the aching space between her thighs, and she yelled, so desperate to have him.

But he had other ideas.

"Tell me you like me." He blew the request across her sex, and her toes curled.

"Never."

A flick of his tongue against her nub made her keen. "Tell me."

"No." But oh, how she wanted to. Biting her tongue though helped her keep the words at bay.

Back and forth they went, him teasing, her denying. He got bolder with his sensual torture and as she panted, every inch of her screaming for release, he demanded she admit her feelings.

She tried to hold on. Tried to chomp off her tongue. *Think nasty thoughts.* Even tried to summon her magic, which slipped through her grasp as he kept teasing her. Wracked with pleasure, mindless with need for him, she finally blurted the words he wanted to hear.

"I love you, dammit. Are you happy now? I don't want to. Oh, how I wish I didn't, but I do."

"Oh, my sweet Ysabel." He growled her name as he raised himself over her. "My very own witch."

The head of his cock unerringly found the entrance to her sex and he thrust. One stroke, two strokes. Her aching flesh molded to his shaft, squeezed around him. She dug her nails into his shoulders as he released her hands. Clung to him as she rode the pinnacle of pleasure. She cried his name when she crested, waves of bliss shuddering through her.

"Oh my beautiful witch, how I love you," he whispered as he thrust one final time, spilling his seed hotly inside her. For a few minutes, she let her resolve slip and allowed herself to believe, to bask in the warmth of his love.

They stayed joined together, breathing erratic, their bodies flushed with sweat. A moment she would always remember as the most beautiful. The most pleasurable. The moment that sealed her fate. *Because now that I've admitted it, he has the power to hurt me.* The thought frightened her to her very core.

THE MOISTURE LEAKING FROM HER EYES SHOCKED HIM. She'd admitted she loved him and now cried. Silently, but still. It wasn't what he'd pictured happening once he admitted his affection.

"What are you doing, witch? Please tell me those are tears of joy."

She pushed at him and he rolled to the side. Up she popped, back ramrod straight, her entire bearing screaming *don't touch*. "I need to be alone."

"Talk to me, Ysabel. What's wrong?"

"You got what you wanted. You made me admit how I feel. Now leave."

"I'm a little confused. I thought being in love was a good thing." He stood from the bed and padded over to her, spinning her to face him.

"A good thing?" She laughed bitterly. "How is it a good thing to fall in love with a demon-whore? How long before you cheat on me and break my heart? A day? Two? Maybe I'll be lucky and you can hide it from me for a few weeks."

"You're it for me, Ysabel. From now until one of us dies. I will touch no other."

"You say it so convincingly," she said, her tone wistful. "But, don't forget, I know all the false promises. I've heard them before. I just don't understand why. I was perfectly fine letting you have your fun with me and then walking. Why did you have to try to make it into something more? Something you know won't last?"

"But I'm telling you the truth." Exasperation colored his words, and still she sadly shook her head. Did she not understand how it worked when a demon mated? That despite their reputation, once they bonded it was one female for life?

"I wish I could believe. Please leave." She pulled away from him, but before he could grab her and shake some sense into her, a furry menace jumped between them. Teeth bared and growling, bloody Felipe dared him to get close enough for a bite.

"Ysabel. Call your cat off."

Turning her back on Remy, his witch instead stalked into the bathroom and the feline stepped closer, still snarling.

"Get the fuck out of my way. I need to talk to her. To make her understand I mean what I say."

It seemed the hellcat wasn't interested in letting him say his piece and given the choice between losing some limbs or hurting her pet, Remy did the only thing he could. He turned on his heel and left.

As he stalked the castle corridors, he tried to figure out where he'd gone wrong. She said she loved him, and he, for the first time, declared himself to a woman. Used the Big L word, and not fallen over dead.

And in the biggest cosmic joke of all, his love made him lose his witch. *How? How is that bloody possible?*

And how can I fix it?

Time to talk to his mother. Surely she had some crazy plan to win over the trust of the one he loved. He just hoped it didn't involve bathing in muds from the Obnoxious Swamp again. The last time it took weeks to get the stench out of his hair and it never did grow him a pair of horns like his mother intended.

Thank Lucifer.

1 2

REMY LEFT without even trying to pit himself against her cat, and Ysabel cried.

Dirty rotten jerk, telling me he loves me.

How dare he raise her hopes? How dare he get to her to admit she cared? Killing him was looking like a better and better prospect all the time, if only she could muster the strength to do so.

I can't do it. I can't end his life. Cowardly of her and weak, yet, she just had to think of his beautiful eyes and earnest expression to lose the fortitude. But, she did have a friend who might help her out.

Heading to Nefertiti's tower, Ysabel caused the damned roaming the streets, and even the demons in her way, to dive to the side for cover. Perhaps it was the scowl on her face or the electrical static making her hair dance or the fireballs she kept lobbing – a corporal manifestation of her turmoil. Whatever the reason, no one dared to say a word or stand in her path as she made the short trek to visit her friend.

Rapping at the tower door – and admiring the new knocker shaped like a man on his knees with his arms bound behind his back – she tapped a foot impatiently as she waited. It took only a short moment before the ornate portal swung open to reveal the handsome figure of Geoffrey, the butler, standing at attention. Literally.

Naked but for a loincloth that did little to hide his straining erection, a must for the staff in this place, Geoffrey bowed her in.

"If my lady witch would follow me, Mistress awaits in the garden."

Spinning on one heel, the butler walked down the corridor, the muscles of his shapely ass flexing. Normally, she would have allowed herself to admire such a prime specimen, even if she would never think of touching, however, consumed with thoughts of Remy, all she could think was how her demon sported a much better set of glutes.

Ruined. He'd ruined her to the point she couldn't even admire another male. With anger now a companion to her misery, she stalked into the garden and found Nefertiti sitting at a wrought iron bistro set, sipping a lemonade while watching her gardener – who wore nothing but a straw hat, a tiny loin cloth and a set of shears. Averting her gaze, Ysabel sat across from her.

"Hey, Nef."

"Ysabel. You naughty devil. A little imp told me someone got lucky last night, but judging by your smile it mustn't have been very good. I'm surprised. Remy has impeccable technique. Or so I've heard. I never tried him out myself. Apparently, belonging to a harem doesn't appeal. His loss."

Ysabel's fingers clawed at the table top as she fought to prevent herself from flying across the table and tackling her friend for even daring to think of Remy in a sexual manner. As to her query…she'd not come here to discuss her bedroom antics, but knowing Nefertiti, if she didn't say something, she'd find a way to pry it out of her. "We had sex. It was good," she grouchily admitted.

"So why the angry face? Did he screw you and run?"

"No."

"Make you swallow when you told him you preferred to spit?"

Cheeks flaming, Ysabel bit out another, "No."

"Did he try to insert his big tool into an out hole?"

"No."

"Then what has your panties in a twist? I don't think I've seen you this miffed since Lucifer bought you that vibrating chair that liked to grope."

Ah, the chair. She'd retaliated for that prank by electrifying his. Not that it worked like expected. Instead of bellowing or shooting smoke from his ears, her boss thanked her with a sly, 'My pubes have never been curlier. Thanks.' She'd had to skip lunch and dinner that day after that admission. It still made her shudder.

Snapping out of the unwanted recollection, she caught Nefertiti's questioning stare. Damn, she still wanted a reason for her annoyance. "He told me he loved me."

Nefertiti blinked. Frowned. Opened her mouth, then closed it again. She shook her head. Slapped her left ear and said, "I'm sorry. Could you repeat that? I could have sworn you said he confessed to loving you."

"He did."

Eyes wide, expression stunned, her friend leaned back in her chair. "Congratulations."

"Excuse me. Did you not hear what I said? The jerk said he loved me."

"Yes. That's quite the feat. I wagered he'd wait until he started going gray in a few hundred years before he'd fall into that trap."

"He hasn't. He's just saying that."

A crease marred Nef's forehead. "Now I'm confused again. Are you saying he's lying about confessing he loves you?"

"Yes. It's part of his ruse."

"Ruse? What kind of ulterior plan could he have?"

"I don't know, but I'm sure I won't like it," Ysabel grumbled.

"Let's skip his confession for a moment. What about you? Do you love him?"

"Yes, the miserable bastard."

Nefertiti's eyes crossed and she closed them as she took a deep breath. "Maybe I'm finally getting slow with old age –"

"Never mistress!" shouted a male voice.

" – but I fail to see the source of your anger. He loves you. You love him. Isn't there a happily ever after in there somewhere?"

"No!"

"Why ever not?" Nefertiti replied in an exasperated tone.

"I know the answer," sang a familiar voice.

Ysabel groaned and put her head down on the tabletop.

"Jallayna," Nefertiti exclaimed. "What a pleasant surprise. I hear congratulations are in order."

"Yes, I won the bet against all those wagering against me. My Remy has finally found a witch crazy enough to make him fall in love. Isn't it wonderful?"

"You're both nuts," Ysabel muttered.

"Thank you," they replied in tandem.

Raising her head, she peered at the two women. "Why is it you both believe he loves me?"

They shared a conspiratorial look. Then shrugged.

"Remy's never said the L word before. Or so my sources say," Nefertiti said.

"And I told you that you were the first girl he's brought home," his mother added.

"So what? I'm supposed to just believe he's going to give up screwing everything with a hole between its legs and settle down with me?"

Dual nods answered her.

And she wanted to believe them. But...

"Oh, don't you dare compare him to Francisco!" Nef exclaimed. "Remy is nothing like that two-faced bastard."

"My boy has honor," Jallayna said with pride. "He also has manners. Why, he never forgets to lift the seat to pee and always puts it down when he's done."

"So you both think I should just throw caution to the wind and let myself believe?"

"It's time you trusted again," Nef said softly.

"You cannot live in fear forever. After I accidentally killed Remy's father, I was crazy with grief for a long time. And when Jacko came along, I also didn't want to let myself love. But he wore me down, and now, even though I'm still slightly insane, I couldn't be happier." Remy's mother beamed. "Oh and my husband says thank you for getting me up to date on the latest fashion trend. He loves my new pantyless state."

Ysabel left as Nefertiti and Jallayna discussed the merits of going around bare-assed. It wasn't a conversation she could have, especially not with Remy's mom. But while the woman seemed to own no personal boundaries, she and Nef had given her food for thought.

Am I being foolish? Is it time I stopped wallowing in fear and let myself trust again? The worst that could happen was Remy breaking her heart. But the best was living with the male she loved. Never being alone. Enjoying laughter in her life again. Surely the benefit, even if it proved temporary, was worth the risk?

She owed it to herself to stop being such a chicken about love. Sometimes a girl got stuck with a loser who broke her heart. Yet, sometimes a witch hit the jackpot, and should enjoy the riches while they lasted. And besides, there were spells to make penises fall off if a man dared stray. But how to tell him? *I wonder if I scared him away permanently with my hissy fit.*

If he truly loved her as he said, then he wouldn't let a temper tantrum stop him. Entering the castle, still lost in her thoughts, it took her a moment to register the imp flitting in front of her.

"What is it?"

"You've got mail," it giggled, thrusting an envelope at her. She snatched it from the clawed paw, but before she could ask who sent it, the mischievous creature flitted away.

The sealed red envelope bore only her name. She

checked it for traces of magic but found none. She sliced it open and pulled out the missive inside.

Ysabel read the note twice, sure she'd misunderstood, but no, there was no mistaking the message.

We've got your demon lover. Either you find a way to get us out of going back to Hell or we'll kill him. Painfully. Do nothing, and we'll still kill him. And then we'll disappear. Hope you enjoy burning alive for an eternity.

Wishing I could watch you burn, again

Francisco

Rotten, fucking bastard. As if she'd let him escape. However, the part that truly made her blood run cold was the threat. *He's got Remy.* Which surprised her. How did one poor excuse for a damned soul get the drop on a warrior of Remy's calibre? Didn't matter. She needed to do something. Letting Remy die, even if it would solve her dilemma with him, never crossed her mind.

She loved him. He might hurt her. Take her love and stomp on it, but that didn't mean she could let him die. *I have to save him.* But how?

On the mortal plane, her powers were diminished, and by the terms of her contract, she was even weaker against her foes? Or was she? Brain kicking into gear, she placed a phone call to her boss, calling his private line.

"Do you do this on purpose to vex me when I'm doing important things?" he asked curtly.

Judging by the giggle, she could guess what Lucifer did. "Say hi to Gaia for me would you?"

He growled. "This is not funny, witch. What is it now? I already told you, I can't return the curse."

"I know. What I want to know is if all the clauses for it transferred."

A minute later, she hung up, and tapped her chin thoughtfully. Good news, but she still needed more help. Remy's life hung in the balance and she refused to take chances. She made another phone call. Actually two, and then got ready to go to war. And for those who wondered, it involved a short skirt, halter top and heels. Unlike other heroines who saved their men in ripped up jeans looking like a tomboy, Ysabel intended to do it in style, sexy style because if she played her cards right, not only would she end the curse, she'd get to claim a prize.

And I know what I want.

Easy access, a grateful demon, and her bent over, seeing stars.

Finding Francisco proved easy. He sent another imp to guide her. The repulsive, green skinned creature insisted she put on an amulet that checked to make sure she was alone, puny magic that she batted aside with ease.

Grinning at the creature for hire, she said. "It's just little ol' me. Take me to your employer."

The route took them in meandering circles that made her want to shake the imp with impatience. As if such a feeble ply would stop a dedicated tracker. How little Francisco knew.

Arriving hours later at the vacant warehouse on the mortal side, she almost laughed at the classic setting. Did all nefarious deeds have to happen at night in remote areas? Although, given what she wanted to do after the rescue, it would suit her purpose because failure just wasn't an option. She would save Remy. She would send Francisco and his mother back to Hell. And then, she'd do the most dangerous thing of all; she'd give Remy her trust.

A familiar hag greeted her at the door, Luysa, still

wearing her medieval garb consisting of a lace mantilla and black dress. But Ysabel didn't have time to waste with the bitter woman.

"So the slut shows herself. Go tell my son," the matron ordered the imp.

Ysabel chanted a few words and flicked her hand. Encasing the imp in a bubble before it could raise an alarm, she smiled at Luysa's shocked face.

"You're not supposed to be able to do that. The contract says," the matron sputtered.

Ysabel smiled slowly. "The thing is, someone else took over the terms. Surprise!"

"Franci – "

Ysabel quickly spun a second spell and slapped a cone of silence around Luysa before she could finish her shout.

"Normally, I would stay and torture you myself," she said. "But, I have a demon to rescue. Oh, Jallayna!" Out of the shadows behind her, cloaked by magic for their trek, Remy's mother appeared.

"Is she the one who likes to play with fire?" she asked, regarding Luysa with slitted, yellow eyes.

"Yup. She's also the one who's trying to make you lose your bet by keeping Remy and I apart."

Tsking as she approached, Jallayna's eyes lit up with a violent madness that Ysabel found endearing. Now here was a mother in law she could grow to love.

"No one messes with my baby boy."

Mouth open in an inaudible scream, Luysa turned to run, but couldn't escape a mother bent on punishment.

Ysabel waggled her fingers goodbye as Jallayna stalked past her with her prize. "Just remember to bring her back to the prison before lunchtime so Remy doesn't have to barbecue again."

An insane giggle was the reply as Jallayna, with Luysa tucked under one arm, bounded away back in the direction of the portal.

One damned soul down, there was just one to go.

Taking a deep breath, Ysabel marched into the forlorn building. *Time to rescue my demon.*

BEING ALMOST HUMAN SUCKED A BIG HAIRY ONE. HOW DID they stand it, Remy wondered as he tugged at the rope binding his wrists? Rope, of all things, holding a demon of his caliber captive. Well, for at least the next couple of minutes. He'd almost undone the knot that bound him.

I should have read the fine print. Eager to spare Ysabel the pain of her curse, he'd not actually done more than skim the document Lucifer wrote up. He signed his name in blood and congratulated himself on doing the most romantic thing ever. But, it seemed he'd not just gotten the whole set-on-fire daily problem, he'd also inherited the whole, weak like a human schmuck when around the souls involved in the curse.

Not that it would matter in the end. Even if his demon powers were dulled down, and he only had his regular strength and wits to aid him, Remy still intended to prevail. Actually, he couldn't wait to have his fist meet Francisco's smirk.

His annoyance with the other male owed very little to his ignoble capture of Remy after he left his mother's house, lost in thought. A stupid victim of an ambush of a dozen bribed demons – who would so get their asses handed to them when he got back to hell. So what if they carried a grudge because he'd kind of slept with all their girlfriend's in the past? It wasn't his fault they couldn't satisfy their ladies.

But it wasn't all those things that made him angry. Oh no, he'd finally confronted the dark haired asshole with the pretty face who not only touched his witch in the past, he'd also dared to hurt her. *He hurt my Ysabel.* And that was not something he could tolerate. *I will avenge my witch.*

Speaking of whom, Ysabel had to wonder where he'd disappeared to. Did she believe he'd abandoned her after getting her to admit she loved him? Fuck. He hoped not. He'd fought hard for that declaration. Nothing and no one better ruin it.

"Still tied up I see," said Francisco sauntering into view with a sneer. "So much for your reputation as a big bad demon. I have to say, I don't see the big deal."

"That's because you're not looking low enough," Remy replied. "Because it is all about size."

"Ysabel never complained when I took her virginity. She was like a cat in heat."

"Virgin? You never told me she was a virgin," a female voice screeched.

With a sigh of annoyance, Francisco turned to a heavy set woman. "So what if I deflowered her. She was still a witch. And she bespelled me."

Luysa pursed her lips. "I am going to check the doors again. I don't trust those magical wards you bought from that vendor." The matron wandered away leaving Remy alone with the object of his annoyance who checked his watch again.

"I don't think Ysabel was that impressed with your skill in the bedroom. Time is almost up, and she's yet to do a thing to save you."

Well, at least that answered one question. Ysabel knew he'd not run out on her, and he'd spank her if she put herself in danger trying to save him, especially since it would mean getting ridiculed by all the other demons.

"Release him or else."

Remy groaned as he couldn't help imagining the jests he'd have to put up with. What male allowed himself to get saved by his woman? "What are you doing, Ysabel? I have this under control."

"Really, because from here it looks like you're all tied up." She strode into view with a cool smile, wearing an outfit that would look even better on the floor.

"Bah, as if something like rope could hold me." He yanked his arms apart and showed her his freed hands, a moment before a sharp point pressed against the back of his neck.

"Move and he dies!" Francisco yelled.

Cocking a hip, and crossing her arms, a smirk crossed his witch's lips. "I don't think so. That demon belongs to me, and I'd prefer him in one piece. So move the dagger away before I hurt you. Or don't. But know this, if you even so much as scratch him, I'll make sure your return to Hell is even more painful."

"I knew you cared," Remy exclaimed.

"Apparently, the insanity in your family is contagious," she replied dryly. "Besides, you already forced me into admitting I loved you. As such, I realized I couldn't exactly let Francisco kill you. That should be my pleasure alone."

"You say the sweetest things," Remy teased.

"But I taste even sweeter," she sassed back.

Despite the knife at his throat, Remy got hard remembering. Time to end this.

"Enough!" Francisco shouted. "Either you get Lucifer to let me go or loverboy here gets it."

Had the little bastard interrupted him and his witch as she publicly admitted she cared? Oh, hell no.

Remy jabbed his elbow back, twisted, then ducked as he grabbed Francisco's dagger wielding hand. He twisted it up behind the damned soul's back and shoved him to his knees. "Sorry, my little witch. You were saying something about pleasure and alone time?"

Her lips twitched and mirth shone in her eyes. "I should have let him kill you."

"But then who would love and worship you for an eternity?"

"You don't have to keep saying that."

"Oh I do. And because you seem to have issues believing me, I even got the contract to prove it."

"You what?"

Francisco chose that moment to squirm and scream obscenities. Remy frowned at him. "I was in the middle of something."

"Interruptions are so rude," she agreed as she came to stand by his side. "I'll be by to see you later, Francisco."

"We both will."

"And until we can come and thank you for bringing us together, I've sent my kitty to greet you in your cell. He's been looking forward to meeting you."

Remy laughed. Now there was a witch who'd fit right in with his family.

Ysabel tagged Francisco and didn't even bother to watch as the man she'd once thought she cared for, who'd hurt her so bad, disappeared. It eased Remy's heart to see Francisco meant nothing to her. Less than nothing. But the way she gazed up at Remy... It stole his breath. Stopped his heart.

In her eyes, he could see the fear, but also the love. The need. Time to show her, that to him, she meant everything.

"Before you shower me with kisses for saving you –"

"I think it could be argued that I played a part."

"Not when I retell the story you won't. But we can argue about that later, naked. As I was saying, I have something for you." Remy pulled the sheet of paper out of his back pocket and unfolded it. Initially he'd worried about it being too short. But as Lucifer assured him when he made the contract and binding, the less clauses he put in, the more his promise would stick out.

Handing it to her, he waited. Fidgeted when she didn't say a word. Almost tore it from her grasp. Then stumbled back as she threw herself at him.

I, Remy, the most awesome demon in Hell, do declare to love the witch Ysabel, fiery temper and all, for an eternity. I will never stray. Never betray her trust. Never do anything to cause her pain upon penalty of permanent death.

This I do swear in blood,

Remy

A simple contract, which in its very lack of clauses and sub items, awed her. "You love me that much?"

He peered at her with incredulity on his face. "Of course I love you that much. Would I have done all the things I did if I didn't?"

"Well, you are related to a mad woman."

"Yes, and maybe it's madness for me to love you, but I do. Do you think just any woman would inspire me enough to take on a bloody painful curse. Or put up with the fact you have a giant, demon eating cat. I know you have trust issues, and that I might not have led the kind of life that inspires confidence, but I will show you that you can believe in me. I want you to love me."

"I know you do. And I do love you. Only for you would I come to the rescue wearing nothing to cover my bottom."

His eyebrows shot up. "You came to battle in a skirt without any underwear?"

A slow nod was her answer.

He grinned, then scowled. "You will not do that again. Do you know how many demons live in the sewer and could have looked up your skirt? I won't have them looking at what's mine. On second thought. Throw out all your underwear. I'll lead the purge on the sewers myself so you can stroll around with your girl parts unencumbered for my enjoyment."

"You're insane," she laughed.

"Crazy in love with you," he agreed. "But I do warn you, we'll have to have dinner with my crazy mother at least once a month."

"Or more often. I quite like your mom. She's got a refreshing way of viewing the world."

"Oh fuck. Don't tell me she's already rubbing off," he groaned, as he pulled her into his arms. She snuggled against him. This was where she belonged.

But she did have a question. "As my new…what should I call you anyway? Boyfriend? Demon I sleep with?"

"The following terms are acceptable to me. Yours. Mate. Husband. Divine taster of your –"

She slapped a hand over his mouth. "I'll stick to mate."

"And I'm going with my super, sexy, touch her and die, fabulous cougar, ass kicking witch."

"I dare you shout that five times in a row without stumbling." He did to her eye popping disbelief.

"I told you, I have a very agile tongue."

"I remember." Boy, did she ever and so did her pussy.

"So is there any reason we're still on the mortal plane instead of back at your place fucking like wild animals?"

"Why wait? I didn't come dressed like this for nothing. And I don't see anyone around." She tossed him a coy smile.

"Evil witch," he growled.

"No, this is evil." Pushing away from him, she turned and bent over with her hands braced on her thighs. She peered at him over her shoulder. The smoldering look on his face made her heart race.

"You naughty, naughty witch. What am I going to do with you?"

"Fuck me?"

"Definitely."

"Make me cum?"

"Goes without saying."

"Love me?"

"Forever and ever."

And then he was inside her, stroking her with his hardness, filling her up, touching her, murmuring the words she allowed herself to embrace. They came together in an explosive burst, linked together for all time by contract, choice and most of all love. *A demon and his witch, together, forever.*

EPILOGUE

Grinning like a lunatic, Lucifer turned his attention away from the happy – ugh – couple on his screen. He'd done it. Paired his biggest pain in the ass with an infamous womanizing demon. Doubts at the beginning of his project, 'Increase My Demonic Population', now seemed ridiculous. Screw Cupid and his bow. He, greatest and most evil ruler of all time, obviously possessed a knack for getting people together. Not to mention, freed up a lot of the ladies for other males. Even better, he'd gotten that bloody witch out of his hair. Not for long though, she was too damned good at her job, which meant he'd have to rehire her, probably for more money, but not right away. He'd take a week to enjoy himself first before he let the harridan return.

While she would get to keep her job, Remy, now that he'd settled down, would probably request assignments closer to home. Lucky for him, a training position had just opened up – because Lucifer killed the previous instructor for banging one of his daughters – which would suit him. If he couldn't have Remy in the field, then operatives trained by him would have to suffice. Not to mention, having Remy close to home, *taking care* of his new wife, meant the witch would start popping out little babies anytime. What a powerful mix those two would make. Little demon/witchlings for Hell's ranks. All part of the plan.

With his army decimated in large numbers because of his recent war with Lilith, he needed to rebuild. Getting demon grunts was the easy part though. Those were a dime a dozen, but dumber than rocks. What he needed was more smart, magic wielding soldiers. However, his demons, witches and other magical beings populating Hell seemed determined to avoid each other.

It was up to him, Lord of the Pit, and now King Matchmaker, to get worthy, loyal demons paired with the right female. Forced breeding wasn't an option because as experience showed, couples in love produced the most offspring, at least in the Pit. Gross. Encouraging affection and healthy relationships went so against the grain, however, he couldn't deny results.

Hence his manipulation of events. Who else but Lord of the Underworld could help five prisoners escape with no one the wiser? Sure he used them, but they should count themselves honored as they served a larger purpose. His purpose.

However one couple alone couldn't give him all the children he'd need to create his next generation of defense. More. He needed more powerful matings, which meant a new project. But who next to torture with that crazy little thing called love?

Hearing a shrill giggle – that was borderline insane –

and the shocking "What the fuck?" from his most staid soldier, Lucifer smiled broadly. Oh fuck yeah. He knew just the pair. Next up in his plan, a demon and his psycho. What a challenging match it would be.

If they didn't kill each other first.

He gleefully rubbed his hands. *Time for round two, in Hell's mating game.*

MEANWHILE IN A CELL, SEVERAL LEVELS DOWN IN HELL'S notorious prison, an enormous hellcat licked its paws clean as a bloody heap whimpered in the corner.

Hurt his adopted mama would he?

Shifting to his man shape, Felipe stood over the jerk who'd watched Ysabel burn alive centuries ago. He wished he could have hurt Francisco more. How dare this sniveling piece of crap harm the woman who'd taken in a lonely kitten and given it a loving home?

"Next time you get a chance to escape," he growled. "I'd throw myself in the abyss because if we ever meet again, I won't be so nice."

Morphing back into his furry skin, Felipe sauntered away and debated what to do next. With his mama now mated to a demon capable of caring for her, it looked like he'd have more time to play because unlike Remy, and other idiot males, no woman was ever going to put a leash on him.

The End (of this story)

But the fun continues in A Demon and His Psycho